THE AMERICAN GRAN

THE
AMERICAN
GRANDDAUGHTER

INAAM KACHACHI

TRANSLATED BY **NARIMAN YOUSSEF**

Interlink Books

An imprint of Interlink Publishing Group, Inc.
Northampton, Massachusetts

First American edition published in 2021 by

Interlink Books
An imprint of Interlink Publishing Group, Inc.
46 Crosby Street, Northampton, Massachusetts 01060
www.interlinkbooks.com

Library of Congress Cataloging-in-Publication Data
Names: Kajah'jī, In'ām, author. | Youssef, Nariman, translator.
Title: The American granddaughter / Inaam Kachachi ; translated by Nariman Youssef.
Other titles: Ḥafīdah al-Amrīkīyah. English
Description: First American edition. | Northampton : Interlink Books, 2020. |
Summary: "In her award-winning novel, Inaam Kachachi depicts the American
occupation of Iraq through the eyes of a young Iraqi-American woman, who returns
to her country as an interpreter for the US Army. Through the narrator's conflicting
emotions, we see the tragedy of a country which, having battled to emerge from
dictatorship, then finds itself under foreign occupation. Zeina returns to her war-torn
homeland as an interpreter for the US Army. Her experiences force her to question all
her values"— Provided by publisher.
Identifiers: LCCN 2020042406 | ISBN 9781623718688 (paperback)
Subjects: LCSH: Iraq War, 2003-2011—Fiction. | Women translators—Iraq—Fiction. |
Granddaughters—Iraq—Fiction. | Grandmothers—Iraq—Fiction. | Families—Iraq—
Fiction. | GSAFD: War stories.
Classification: LCC PJ7842.A32738 H3413 2020 | DDC 892.7/37—dc23
LC record available at https://lccn.loc.gov/2020042406

Printed and bound in the United States of America

For Talal

Beware the beautiful woman of dubious descent.

An unauthenticated Hadith

I

If sorrow were a man I would not kill him. I would pray for his long life.

For it has honed me and smoothed over the edges of my reckless nature.

It has turned the world and everything in it a strange color with unfamiliar hues that my words stutter to describe and my eyes fail to register.

Maybe I was color-blind before. Or was my eyesight perfect then, and is the color that I now see the wrong one?

Even my laughter has changed. I no longer laugh from the depths of my heart like I used to, unashamedly showing the crooked line of my lower teeth that Calvin once likened to a popular café in the wake of a brawl. Calvin was flirting in his own way. But flirting no longer suits me now. Who would flirt with a woman who bears a cemetery inside her chest?

Miserable, that's what I've become. A dressing-table turned upside down, its mirror cracked. I laugh joylessly from the outer shell of my heart. A sugar-free laugh, low-cal, like a tasteless soda. Do I even really laugh? I just struggle for the briefest smile. As if I have to repress any possible joys or fleeting delights. I have to keep my inner feelings well covered for fear they'll boil over and reveal the state I've been in since Baghdad.

I came back feeling wrung out, like a rag used to mop the floor. A floor mop. That's what I've become.

I left behind parts of myself I had held on to since childhood. I used to look at what happens around me as a sequence of raw footage, every chapter of my life a movie inviting me to find a suitable title. Now the hardest-hitting movie is running before my eyes and I can't find a title that would possibly fit. I see myself on the screen, a disillusioned saint carrying her belongings in a khaki backpack, wearing a hard helmet and dusty boots and walking behind soldiers who raise the victory sign despite their defeat. Where have I come across this scene before? Was it not also there in Iraq, in a past age, in another life? Are defeated armies bred on the fertile land between those two rivers?

I confess that I returned defeated, laden with the gravel of sorrow and two sweet limes that I craved on my mother's behalf. My mother, who it seems, discovered the saving grace of disappointment long before I did, particularly on that day in Detroit when she pledged allegiance to the United States and attained the boon of its citizenship.

Her eyes welled with tears when I presented her with the green fruit picked from the garden of the big house in which she spent her youth. She took the limes in both hands and inhaled deeply like she was smelling her father's prayer beads and her mother's milk and her past life. A betrayed life encapsulated in two limes.

Yet, I like this sorrow of mine. I feel the softness of its

gravel as I wade with bared soul into its fountain, and I have no desire to shake off its burden. My beautiful sorrow which makes me feel that I am no longer an ordinary American but a woman from a faraway and ancient place, her hand clutching the burning coal of a story like no other.

II

Dil dil dilani,
To Baashika and Bahzani.
Baba went to the old town stall,
Brought us chickpeas and raisins.
He gave them to our nanny
And she ate them all …

Grandma Rahma rocks me back and forth, after settling me on her warm lap with my face towards her. My fragile chest meets her bounteous breasts. They spill out of her white cotton bra, which she boils in water and grated soap whenever it turns yellow with sweat. I look at her, spellbound by the pale rosiness of her face, and cling to her arms. My legs dangle on either side of her, not reaching the sofa on which she's sitting with her knees elegantly touching, in the way she learned from *Eve* magazine. My educated grandmother, who could read and write and follow the press, who seemed a marvel among women of her generation.

She leans forward with me until the world starts to spin in my eyes, then she snatches me back, repeating all the while the old rhymes that engraved their message forever upon my still-soft memory. Rhymes inherited from the days of Mosul and the old stone house that sits on a cliff overlooking the river. The house of Girgis Saour, my great-grandfather whose last name Saour—the churchwarden—he acquired from taking care of Al-Tahira Church, together with its saints' icons and its candlesticks that every Saturday had to be cleaned of the wax that had hardened on the shafts and polished with a slice of lemon.

They took me to Mosul one day when I was little. It was Easter, early April, and the valleys were ablaze with camomile flowers. The sprawling yellow vastness bewitched me, the scent of nature made me dizzy. The wild poppies growing out of the cracks in the rocks were an astonishing sight, as red as the cheeks of my cousins when they walked out of the bathroom with water dripping from their long hair. How could I not love Mosul, when everyone there spoke with my grandmother's accent?

I liked my Mosul relatives, with their shiny backcombed hair and pale rosy faces. They would visit us at Christmas or when they came down to Baghdad to attend to business at a government office or to see a good doctor. They sat silent and worried on the edge of the wooden Thonet-style chairs that were common at the time. They sat as if ever ready to stand up, be it to receive a tea tray, welcome a new arrival or give the seat up to an elder, supporting small paunches with the right hand and running through the beads of a rosary with the left. When they spoke it was as if the kitchen cupboards had collapsed and a cacophony of pots and pans were spilling out. Words rolled out of my relatives' mouths in a burst of *qafs* and *gheins*, with the elongated *alef* at the end making everything sound like the finale of a musical *mawwal*. *Ammaaa … Khalaaa …* They sounded like they had just stepped out of a period drama in classical Arabic extolling the chivalry of Seif Al-Dawla. Even though I loved my Mosul relatives, I never felt fully at home in that big humid house with the stairs that led up to more than one attic and down to many cellars. The steps were too big for my short skinny legs, and the single skylight at the top of the staircase wasn't enough to banish the darkness.

My grandmother's lullaby came back to me as I rode in the convoy along the road from Mosul to its surrounding villages. In Baashika the girls stood in front of their houses adjusting the white scarves on their heads as they watched us pass by. My movie about them would be called *Doves and Handkerchiefs*. The blank expressions on their faces gave nothing away. None of them were smiling or waving their handkerchiefs like in the scenes in my head from American World War II movies of girls in Paris and Naples waving to US Army convoys and climbing onto the armoured vehicles to steal a kiss from the lips of a handsomely tanned soldier.

I told the guys that Baashika was probably an old corruption of "*beit al-ashika*," the lover's house. While Bahzani, the neighboring village, derived from "*beit al-hazina*," the sad woman's house. They applauded these pieces of trivia, but quickly returned to their mood of anxiety as we passed men with thick moustaches, dressed in white with bright scarves, who stepped out from behind the cypresses and threw fiery looks in the direction of our convoy. I wanted to jump off the truck, shout something like "*Allah yesa'edhum!*" and make small talk. Maybe ask about the wheat season or about the nearest store to buy a loofah for the bath, or simply invite myself in for a glass of cold water in one of their houses. I wanted to flaunt my kinship in front of them, show them that I was a daughter of the same part of the country, that I spoke their language with the same accent, I wanted to tell them that Colonel Youssef Fatouhy, assistant to the Chief of Army Recruitment in Mosul in the 1940s, was my grandfather. But all that would've been against orders, unnecessary chatter that could endanger me and my colleagues. Orders demanded I be mute. And so, for the first time, I resented my army uniform that was cutting me off from my people. It made me feel we were crouching in opposing trenches. We *were* in fact crouching in opposing trenches. Like any skilled actor, I felt I had the ability to adopt a role and change character, to be simultaneously their daughter and their enemy, while they could be my kin as well as my enemy.

From that day on, I became aware of the malady of grief that afflicted me, to which I adapted and for which I sought no cure.

For how do I fight a malady that brought about my rebirth,
that fed me and let me grow
and rocked me to sleep,
that honed and educated me,
and disciplined me so well?

III

"Ninety-seven thousand dollars a year. All expenses paid."
That was the mantra that started it all. It spread among
Iraqis and other Arabs in Detroit, setting suns alight underneath
heavy quilts and making palm leaves sway above the snow that
still covered front yards.

Sahira came over, tossed the words like a burning coal into
my hands and left in a hurry without drinking her coffee. I
heard the wheels of her old Toyota screech as she sped away to
carry the good tidings to the rest of her friends and relatives.

This wasn't the kind of thing you could chat about on
your cellphone. A national lottery to be won only by the most
fortunate Arabic-speaking Americans like me and Sahira, who,
when I asked her how she could go and leave her two teenage
sons, simply said: "The boys? They didn't sleep a wink all night
they were so excited. They stayed in my bed and were begging
me to hurry up and register my name before the opportunity
is lost to someone else." Ninety-seven thousand dollars was
enough for children to drive their parents into the battlefield.

Add to that 35 percent danger-money, a similar percentage for hardship and professional welfare, plus a little bit spare here and a little bit there, and the amount could reach one hundred and eighty-six thousand dollars a year. Enough to say goodbye forever to the miserable neighborhood of Seven Mile, enough to make a down payment on a grand house in the heart of leafy Southfield and purchase a new car. Enough also to send my brother Yazan, now Jason, to drug rehab, and then support him through college.

One or two years. Then things would settle down. My mother's lungs would be cleansed of the cheap cigarette smoke she'd been inhaling every night, year after year, while she sobbed in her room. I could hear her through the wooden walls. Sometimes she sobbed soundlessly, like a broken TV, but later I would see her wet cheeks and learn that women didn't cry from loneliness alone, but also from want. Money was a form of happiness. And I would bring happiness to my mother. I wouldn't let this opportunity pass me by.

In the days that followed Sahira's visit, private companies contracted by the Department of Defense started spreading the news in immigrant communities, on the internet, on local TV, and through word of mouth after Sunday mass in the churches of Detroit and Chicago and even in the Shia mosques of Dearborn.

As if at the touch of a magic wand, an endless emporium of bid and counterbid, tips, schemes and three-card tricks laid out its wares. There were those who offered encouragement, applauding and embellishing the experience, and those who looked away, spitting warnings against the betrayal of the land from whose Tigris and Euphrates we had drunk, even if it was for the good of our new land that poured us Coca-Cola morning and night.

The war was about to begin, and there was talk of nothing else. We heard the drums of war beating in newspaper headlines and Congressional speeches, on the flags popping up on front lawns, in the planes passing overhead, and the ships assembling their crews to carry them to warmer waters.

So, on one of my identical mornings, instead of starting my automatic round of tidying the house, I sat down, dialed the number of one of the companies recruiting Arabic-speaking translators and left the details required. I wasn't afraid of the war or of dying or returning with a disability. There was no time to think about such real things in the midst of the raucous carnival of excitement. I repeated after Fox News that I was going on a patriotic mission. I was a soldier stepping forward to help my government, my people and my army, our American army that would bring down Saddam and liberate a nation from its suffering.

I pulled into the spacious parking lot in front of Walmart, but instead of getting out of the car, I sat still and watched the snowflakes on the windshield. I no longer needed to buy a blouse or a new pair of shoes. From now on my clothes would be different. Resting my arms on the steering wheel, I saw a soldier in army uniform walking across the parking lot under the falling snow, heading towards the honor that awaited her only a dream or two away, there, in the country of my birth.

The poor people of Iraq. They won't believe their eyes when they finally open onto freedom. Even old men will become boys again when they sup from the milk of democracy and taste of the life I lead here. These were the kind of thoughts glowing in my head and almost lighting up my car. The glow intensified in unison with the idea of the one hundred and eighty-six thousand dollars, the price of my precious language, the price of my blood.

What did patriotism feel like? A load of nonsense that never meant much to me, neither during my Iraqi childhood nor during my American youth. Then came 9/11 and it was like an electric shock sending its energy through the bodies of all my friends and neighbors. We turned into creatures that shook and trembled, emitting sounds of panic and indignation, clasping hands above heads or using them to cover mouths. "Oh my God... Oh my God," ceaselessly repeated, as if the rest of the language had been forgotten and these three words were all that remained.

I had woken up that morning, as usual, to the sound of my mother coughing in her bedroom. It wasn't yet seven. Like a robot executing its pre-programmed morning routine, I headed for the kitchen to put water in the electric coffee machine; then to the living room to tidy the newspapers and cushions; then to Yazan's room to wake him up; then back to the kitchen to prepare his school lunch, before finally settling with my coffee—cradling the mug with both hands—in front of the TV to watch the news. Things that I did half-asleep, my hands moving without the need to engage my brain. But on that day I went straight from my bed to the TV and reached for the remote while I was still standing. I don't know what impulse diverted me from my usual routine. Perhaps someone had put a bug in the robot's program the night before.

I watched a plane crashing into a tower. There was another tower burning right next to it on the screen.

I froze where I stood. I knew these two buildings. I knew New York. Every American did. Whether or not she'd ever been there. I had visited New York, stood in front of her Twin

Towers and had a bite to eat on the plaza that led to one of them. Yes, there used to be an Iranian selling kebab from a cart at the foot of the World Trade Center.

I remained frozen, not blinking, not breathing, not registering what I was seeing. The only thing moving was my finger pressing the remote. I turned up the volume to find out if this was a movie or a special effects scene being shot, but my eyes fell immediately on the phrase "Breaking News" at the bottom of the screen. America was on fire before my eyes, and I could smell the ash. The name of this movie has got to be *The Towering Inferno*.

A week later, the FBI was recruiting Arabic translators and advertising a web address for applications. I read the ad and felt a mixture of vulnerability and enthusiasm. What could I do to help my country in its adversity? How could a powerless immigrant like me serve the great United States of America? It was impossible to remain indifferent after witnessing that inferno, impossible to be content with my small hopes and to continue living with my mother's coughing and my brother's drugged stupor. Quickly, without thinking too much—which would've changed little anyway—I filled out an online application. It wasn't a rash decision. I knew exactly what I was getting into.

Another week passed before I received a phone call from Washington, DC to go and take the assessment. Now one thing I was confident about was the flawlessness of my Arabic. I'd caught the language like a contagion from my Assyrian father. He never used to buy me toys, because our favorite game was Poetry Pursuit. He would recite a verse of poetry that ended, say, on the letter *nun*, and I would have to reply with a line starting with the same letter. Sometimes when I got stuck I would make something up, and he would pinch my earlobe and repeat the religious saying, "Those who cheat are not of us," then add, "But exceptions can be made for little poetesses."

Apart from Calvin, I mostly mixed with Arabs. "You, my darling, represent the white minority in our midst." He liked that joke, just as he liked everything I said, mostly. My Calvin, my poor, unassuming, drunk Calvin, unemployed most months of the year and who, when I raised my voice in conversation with friends, would think we were fighting.

"Don't worry, honey. It's just politics."

"Politics, always politics!"

At home I never heard my mother speak anything but Iraqi Arabic, although my father wanted us to learn Chaldean too, his mother tongue. English remained the language of the street, work and the news. We would contort our jawbones and speak it the moment we stepped outside the house. Our cars took us and our English around from street to street and from mall to mall. Then they brought us back to the zinc covered garages in front of the house, where we changed language again and slipped indoors.

"How come your daughter hasn't forgotten the language of your country?" the neighbors would ask when they heard me chatting on the phone to Sahira, and my mother would smile and look at me with a pride that bordered on gratitude. How she wished she could have given me the last name of her respected Mosul family: Zeina Behnam *Saour*. If only my destiny had led there and I'd married one of my maternal cousins. Or if I'd carried my mother's last name alongside my father's on my ID, like Spanish women did. Oh, the hopes of Sitt Batoul, and her stubbornness and her constant arguing with my dad. Wasn't he the one who deserved credit for my language, that jewel around my neck that was the source of her pride?

Something, perhaps divine good fortune, stopped me forgetting how to read and write in Arabic after we left Baghdad. There was, of course, Hermes, my sensitive friend from Alqosh, my closest and most loyal guy friend. A poet in the style of Nizar Qabbani, Hermes wrote plays and stories in Arabic and asked me for feedback on what he wrote. Lots of books and novels came for him by mail, ordered from a bookshop in Dearborn or from online stores. He'd devour them like fast food then pass them on to me. I loved to read slowly, savoring the weight of every word. I would read aloud, as my grandfather would do when I was little holding the newspaper in front of him while my grandmother listened. My father too liked to read aloud. That was his job, and it put food on our table, but then that turned into poison.

Like all immigrants in our community, the corners of our apartment—one of four apartments that made up a derelict wooden building in Seven Mile—were also piled high with cassette tapes and CDs of Arabic songs by Fairuz, Um Kulthum, and Kazim Al-Sahir. Plus, I had my gang in Detroit. The movie about us would be called *Zeina's Gang*. That's how my mom referred to my group of Lebanese, Iraqi, Palestinian, and Syrian friends. There was one Egyptian woman among us, and she never tired of talking about the plays of Mohammad Sobhy, which meant nothing to me at the time. My gang met for dinner on the first Saturday of every month at one of the Arabic restaurants in the city. We chatted and laughed, ate taboulah, mejaddarah and shawermah, and danced to the rhythms of the oud and tabla. That was the one evening that Calvin eagerly awaited to take a break from me.

So of course I passed the language test.

I waited for them to contact me but they took their time and the war started without me. I heard on the news that the president had secured the support of Congress. Who cared about the United Nations? What nations and what bullshit? With the start of operations, we all became slaves to the TV screens. We were addicted to the news and never got our fill. If you nodded off in front of the screen, dozens of hands would shake you awake. If you sleep, you miss out on history!

Despite my enthusiasm for the war, I experienced a strange kind of pain that was hard to define. Was I a hypocrite, a two-faced American? A dormant Iraqi like those sleeping cells of spies planted in an enemy land and lying in wait for years? Why did I suddenly go all Mother Theresa—the namesake of my patron saint—over the Iraqi victims? I collapsed into myself as I watched Baghdad being bombed and the columns of smoke rising after each American attack. It was like watching myself use my mom's cigarette lighter to set my own hair on fire, or cut my own skin with my nail scissors, or slap my left cheek with my right hand.

Why couldn't I sit still for five minutes? I told that other who was also me that there were terrified children and inno-cent civilians dying in Baghdad. I told her those children could be the children of your classmates from school, and the dead civilians could be the sons of your uncles or the daughters of your aunts. That charred body at the entrance of Al-Karkh Hospital might be Suheil, the son of your neighbor Sitt Lamiaa, the boy who kissed you on the roof of your house in Ghadir. Have you forgotten your very first kiss, on the day you'd gone up to the roof to watch the solar eclipse, clutching in your hands the cardboard sunglasses that had come with the day's newspaper? You were not yet ten.

The TV wouldn't stop charging us with emotion. It pumped us with adrenaline as it carried images of smoke and the noise of explosions, scenes of men running to escape death, and of boys yellow-faced with panic but waving victory signs to the cameras all the same. I watched people enter government buildings and leave with tables and chandeliers and chairs and plastic plants carried on their heads or their backs. Everyone racing for a share of the pillage. Some laughed at the camera when they realized they'd been caught unawares, but the majority looked away and rushed on. Baghdad had become a free for all. Iraq was leaderless.

But in spite of everything I saw, I wasn't afraid or tempted to withdraw. So when Sahira came and threw that burning coal into my lap, I applied again. I didn't wait long this time, but soon received a phone call from a man who didn't introduce himself. He gave me a sentence to translate into Arabic as a quick phone test, and asked a few questions about my age, qualifications, health and social and financial status. He wanted to make sure the applicant wasn't in debt and just after the money. I answered all of his questions calmly and with few words, trying all the time to visualize his face. I don't know why I attached the face of Sean Connery to his voice: I was applying for work as an interpreter, not as a secret agent. It seemed that my calmness persuaded him that I was suitable for the job, because he asked me to come in for a meeting and, two days later, sent me a plane ticket to the capital.

I said goodbye to Mom and Jason and traveled on a gray morning to Washington, DC, joining dozens of other Arabs who had applied for the same work. From there I called my dad in Arizona and told him that I was going to Baghdad. At first he said nothing, then he mumbled a few words from which I gathered that he didn't like the idea, not because of the war but because he imagined that his death sentence was still in effect and feared they might arrest me in his place.

That was it then: CIA headquarters in Virginia.

A place that was the subject of whispered stories became my daily destination. It was no longer a mystery hidden behind green walls and tall, well-maintained trees. It was just an assortment of offices and ordinary employees, among them clever ones who could read my facial expressions and stupid ones who spent their days scratching their balls and waiting for the pay check at the end of the month.

They put me through detailed interviews and made me sit through lectures on the nature of the job, showed me maps and films explaining the geography of Iraq, and sent me for a full medical. I wasn't alone in that bizarre carnival. Translation agencies were multiplying and producing dozens of applicants every day. There were Iraqi men and women from different sects and backgrounds. Some were relatively recent migrants who had come to the United States from Rafha camp after the invasion of Kuwait, others were veteran migrants who had arrived here in the 1960s in search of economic gain, and yet others were "in-betweeners," '70s migrants who had escaped the Baathist prosecution of communists and headed for Eastern Europe, somehow ending up in the mecca of capitalism. There was a strange mix of Americanized Islamists, and leftists who mislaid Moscow's compass. Some were vain and showy performers, while others were introverts, but each and every one looked fit for a part in a movie I'd call *I Ain't Got No Work*. There were veiled women and girls in tight jeans, men with Stalinist moustaches, young men with heads shaved like rap artists. Not all were Iraqis. Some of the would-be translators were from other Arab countries, others were Arabized foreigners.

We each filled out a thick folder of forms, answering questions about every single member of the family, their ages, their addresses, their past and current nationalities. I heard former Baathists joking among themselves that those "lists" were like the lists the regime in Iraq used to demand from its followers. Your name, your and your brother's political leanings, your father's pants size, your sisters' eye colors, and the addresses of all your relatives, to the seventh remove. I took my time answering everything and paid attention to my handwriting. There was a question about relatives in Baghdad, to which I answered that my maternal grandmother lived in Baghdad and that she was my only family there.

My grandmother, Rahma Girgis Saour. I transliterated her name into English, and under date and place of birth, I wrote: 1917, Mosul.

IV

Cheeeeese.

The photographer gave his standard instruction for us to show our teeth. We all followed like actors in a Colgate ad and smiled for the camera. Less than a week later, the photograph would be delivered to us, enlarged and in transparent wrapping. We would grab it eagerly and make various comments as we pass it around. I would then carry it carefully to my room and put it in the expensive frame that I'd bought especially from the home accessories section at Macy's. It would finally settle on the mantelpiece in our living room, displaying the four of us formally dressed and posing in the garden of our house on the day that we became Americans. How we had waited for that day!

Looking at that picture, it's easy to see that my father had dressed up especially for the occasion in his dark blue suit, the one made by Mujawwadi, the tailor in Baghdad's new market. As for the slim blond boy—my brother Jason—and the dark-skinned young woman who looked like she was borrowed from another family—me—we had both worn without argument what Mom had told us to. She was the only one not dressed up. She hadn't passed the thin black kohl pencil along her upper eyelids, the only make-up that she normally wore. She had on her old blue baggy dress, the one that usually meant it was a major cleaning day. Our protests had done nothing to change her mind. "Stubbornness is a birthmark that Batoul was born with. God-given." That was what Grandma used to say about her eldest, my mother.

So Batoul wasn't dressed and made up for the occasion like the thousands who filled the area surrounding Wayne State University in Detroit. The city council had lined the street with thousands of chairs, and the happy crowds of Arabs, Puerto Ricans, Chinese and Indians came and took over the place. All were in their best attire, as though it were a holiday, but even more special than a holiday, for this was more unique.

My mother walked apart from us, looking like she was in a funeral procession. She sat huddled up and hugged her handbag like there was something in it she was sheltering. She glanced sideways at her neighbors in the surrounding seats who couldn't contain their excitement. It was their collective wedding. The moment that would banish their fears and drive away forever the specter of homelessness. The day they swore allegiance to their new bounteous homeland. After the oath, they would be entitled to push out their chests and boast: "I am an American citizen."

As the loudspeakers echoed the voice of the state governor reading out the oath of allegiance, as the crowd of men and women stood up, raised their voices in unison and—with all the passion and assertiveness they could muster—repeated the words after him, as the newly baptized Americans hugged each other and exchanged congratulations, I heard my mother's voice break as if she were suffocating... I turned to her and she looked like she'd been attacked by a sudden fever. Her pale face had turned purple and tears streamed down from her eyes and seemed to evaporate on touching her burning cheeks, like water dripping from the teapot onto a hot stove.

I reached out and took her stiff hand in mine. The masses put their hands on their hearts and sang out the national anthem as the jazz band started playing: "God Save America. God Bless America." The voice of my mother, the Iraqi woman Batoul Fatouhy Saour, was the only one out of tune, as she wailed in Arabic, "Forgive me, Father. *Yaabaa*, forgive me."

What on earth had brought Grandpa Youssef to University Street in Detroit?

V

It was the day for preparing army uniforms.

Pushing a trolley in front of me, I stood in a long line of women and men, like in a supermarket. Except we weren't browsing shelves stacked with tinned food and cartons of milk. We were headed for the clothes warehouse. Tables were spread out in front of shelves packed with folded clothes. Khaki pants and shirts, shoes and socks, belts, woollen underwear. We were brides and the army was in charge of our wedding trousseaux. I followed what everyone in the line in front of me was doing, reaching up to the shelves, pulling out clothes in my size and putting them in my cart. Our measurements had been taken the day before so we knew what to pick.

One of five days of preparations that preceded our departure.

As soon as we arrived in the camp, they roll-called our names. Zayna Behnaym. That's how they pronounced my name. I moved forward, and they checked my identity and gave me a sheet, a pillow and a blanket. I carried my gear under my arm and walked to where the bedrooms were. Each room slept four or five. The following day was for medical checks. Army doctors were no different from other doctors except they were in uniform. Another day was for filling out official forms with personal data. Did my life really contain all I was being asked to recall?

To get to the camp I'd taken a civilian plane from Detroit. There was an army bus waiting for us at the airport. The moment I placed my right foot on the bus steps, I realized that I was folding away all my past life. Everything before me was a brand new page, and from this moment onwards my life would no longer be the same. The girl who had grown up watching her dreams burst like balloons at the end of a birthday party was going to war. The silly girl who'd cried more than once over failed loves was about to join the US Army.

I didn't give in to my daydreams for long. It wasn't a time for such indulgence. My bus companions were letting off steam through forced cheerfulness, laughing about everything and nothing. I knew that laughter wasn't necessarily a sign of happiness. Benjamin, the cleaner at the Assyrian Club in Baghdad, was given to laughing non-stop after his son was killed in the Kurdish war. After a while I stopped seeing him, and then I learned that he was taken to Al-Shamiya psychiatric hospital.

There were two other women on the bus, an Egyptian and a Lebanese. I could tell from their accents. The Egyptian, who was a hustler by nature, commanded the scene and demanded attention. She told me, later on, how she'd cast her net over an American visiting Alexandria, and how he'd married her and brought her to his country. She acquired citizenship and left her husband after she got pregnant with the child of a Cuban pizza delivery guy. She was joining the translators and leaving her nursing baby behind with her ex-husband. She was dark and plump with long hair and jittery movements. I liked her openness and felt that we could be friends.

The Lebanese had two suitcases with her, each as big as a city and filled with beautiful clothes and cosmetics. She said that her name was Rula. She sat on the bus, with her legs crossed elegantly, and looked like she was going on honeymoon to Paris.

Nadia, the Egyptian who shook every time she laughed with an invisible electric current that ran through her pores, was telling Rula that she wanted to work in one of the fabulous palaces in the Green Zone. Everything to her was "fabulous." I heard Rula answer that she'd refuse to stay anywhere except the Baghdad Hotel. How did she know about the Baghdad Hotel? She curled her full upper lip and said, "Even if they don't pay for the hotel I'll pay out of my own money." How deceptive the dreams of adventure could be! How could this pampered girl have known that we were going to sleep in the arms of death and seek shelter in our coffins? I myself didn't know, nor did Sahira or Captain Donovan, or Brian, whose body would be found floating among the weeds of the Euphrates.

We got up at 5 a.m. to join the queue for registration. Our routine was becoming more like that of a military camp. Everything around us was rough and masculine, and we weren't yet trained for it. But it wouldn't do to cling on to femininity. Here you were either a soldier or a concubine.

We stood in line with the soldiers. They in their army khaki and we still in our civilian clothes, tight jeans, and high heels. I was surprised to see the other girls had found the time to paint their lips and apply coats of mascara. At what hour had those killer eyes woken up?

The following day I got my army uniform with my name stitched into it. For reasons of personal safety, they gave us the choice between using our real family names or any other. The tight jeans and high heels were gone. We were no longer distinguishable from the soldiers at the camp. I took comfort from this. It was a tangible sign of my new character: intrepid Zeina going to war.

Then came the day of our departure.

VI

The words filling my head are white clouds taking flight. They move and merge and change shapes, and then all at once they stop and pour forth their acid rain. My fingers race on the keyboard, trying to capture the images before they disperse like white clouds chased by the wind.

I write knowing that death could come at any moment. In the form of a roadside bomb, or a mortar shell that drops on my head inside the Green Zone and leaves me burning like a matchstick. Will I live to finish this story that's not mine as much as it is hers? My grandmother, my enemy, my beloved, the image of my old age.

I ignore the author who's intruding on my space at the computer, sitting shoulder to shoulder by my side, as if we were a duet forced to play on one piano. She wants us to type to-gether—four hands, twenty fingers—the story of the American granddaughter returning to the family home in Baghdad. But I don't want her by my side. I push her away and fight against her persistence. I keep pressing the backspace key, deleting the words she writes.

She's getting on my nerves, circling and maneuvering in order to force out a patriotic novel at my expense. The impostor wants to kill me off so she can win for herself the admiration of idiotic critics, TV politicians and dinosaur nationalists. She wants to paint me as the villain and my grandmother as the brave and kind heroine, something like the actress Amina Rizk in the Egyptian film *Nasser*: a woman of principles, who, when her grandfather dies in forced labor at the Suez Canal, refuses to receive mourners until the Free Officers take over in the July revolution and she believes his death has been avenged.

The author sees me as a step-daughter of the occupation and my grandmother as a jewel of the resistance. I am the sinning Magdalene who deserves to be stoned and my grand-mother an immaculate virgin in her eighties. She gives me the features of the prodigal daughter who returns like a female Rambo on a US Army tank. She traps me twice—inside the Green Zone and inside a hateful character—and imposes her unreconstructed nationalist imagination on me, an imagination inherited in black and white and sepia, no longer suitable for the age of Photoshop. But her traps neither impress nor interest me. Her weak narrative plot tries to silence me and rob me of my right to have a say in the affairs of this land that witnessed my birth and the births of my parents. Why does she want to prevent me from participating in the story in my own way, with full commitment and without a prompter feeding me the lines, hidden off-stage?

I bet it's because she herself has only ever known the words of prompters. She's never written one sentence of her own making, never tasted the joy of expressing what's really on her mind, out loud and without fear of a raised rough hand that could descend on her soft cheek with a slap to reprimand the digression. She's conditioned to reject her own reason, to believe blindly in the intimations of the heart and to accept rhetoric and poetry as keys to the undisputed truth.

How can I make her understand that I'm stronger than she is? That I pity her naivety and lament her rancid, Stone Age nationalism. I won't allow her to write about me. I'll tell her, in all honesty, that I nearly die laughing at her passion for slogans, her blindness and her grand sense of mission that turns her novels into rowdy demonstrations chanting pre-written slogans. Long live this. Down with that.

I'm not going to play along. Let the author go to hell!

I'll even incite Rahma against her. My grandmother is a wise woman who doesn't fall into traps that easily. She wouldn't be comfortable in the veil of a Virgin Mary or the galabiyya of Amina Rizk. She'd refuse to leave her own nationalism in the hands of a writer who's so mired in the worlds of revolutionary coups and nationalistic parties; she made them into her own paper trumpet. No. I won't let my grandmother hand over my grandfather's history.

Oh God, how much I intersect with that history, and how we diverge!

It is my history, whether I like it or not. It was mine even before I was born. I am its legitimate child, no matter how foreign I may seem. How dare she, that gullible author, think that I'll just hand over my inheritance to her, even if that inheritance is nothing but a tattered piece of nationalism, good for nothing, a handful of coins in a currency that went out of circulation a long time ago?

VII

At the Rhein-Main military airport near Frankfurt, I took out my laptop and wrote the first email to Calvin since leaving Detroit. "We are at the airport in Germany. The smell of beer that fills the transit lounge made me think of you … please don't drink too much … and don't worry about me … don't forget to water my plants … and if I'm gone too long and you decide to love another woman, make sure she's not an Iraqi this time … you've suffered enough for one lifetime!"

We'd flown to Germany in a civilian plane and from there the military aircraft that were constantly coming and going took charge of our transportation to Iraq, each plane taking as many passengers as its space permitted. For the first time in my life I boarded a plane from its backside. For that's how the C-17 opens, from the back, its mouth is wide like the jaws of a shark. I was contemplating the aircraft, and thinking about having my photo taken next to it, when a strong hand pushed me towards the steps. Where were the seats? It was a huge and ugly cargo plane with connected benches along its walls. Our bags were piled up in the middle and secured to the ground with belts to prevent them from sliding. Even those were nothing like ordinary luggage, but khaki-green canvas bundles with long zippers. Looking around me, I counted twenty-nine individuals about to share the stressful journey. Five of us were women. They'd given us yellow earplugs to block the roaring noise of the plane, but they only worked to a certain extent. We couldn't hear each other throughout the five-hour-long flight, so we flew in a silence that was charged with anticipation and anxiety. Every now and then someone would make a hopeful attempt to dispel the tension by forcing small talk, but they were like actors in a silent movie, their voices lost to the roar of the engines.

We were each given a lunch box. I opened mine and found a sandwich, a bag of potato chips, a coke and a cookie. We ate like savages. As soon as we finished, the captain announced that we were going to refuel mid-air, and warned us that we might experience an uncomfortable feeling. The fuel plane mounted ours and remained there for about half an hour. There was severe turbulence as soon as the two planes touched, and I started to feel sick. The title for this movie could be *Damsels in Distress and Helpless Knights*. None of us was trying to play Rambo. That would've been a different movie altogether. I was terrified the fueling might cause the plane to explode, but it went okay, and, more importantly, I didn't throw up. I wasn't alone in letting out a sigh of relief when that episode was over. We exchanged smiles, as we were too paralyzed to shake hands.

Eventually we landed.

Despite the anxiety and tiredness, I was overtaken by a strange sense of transcendence as soon as we entered Iraqi airspace. I imagined I could smell the blossoms of Seville oranges on the garden trees and the delicious scent of the smoke cooking *masgoof* fish. This state lasted for only a minute or so before the headlights of the plane were switched off and we were hovering over Baghdad, preparing to land. I felt the terrible injustice of this darkness. The blinds had to be closed as well, blocking the city from my view completely. With all these precautions, I remembered my mother's fears as she read about the missiles that targeted planes trying to land in Baghdad. If she were here she'd tell me to pray.

Holy Mary. Please let us arrive safely, oh sweet Maryam.

When the plane finally landed, and the roar of the engines stopped, it was like I'd suddenly gone deaf. I got to my feet, feeling like a granite statue that had just come to life, then lost my balance and fell back onto my seat. I got up again and followed the others off the plane. As the huge back door was slowly lowered, my eyes panned like a camera from left to right, trying not to miss anything of those first moments. But all I could see was something like a red curtain that was covering the door of the aircraft from outside. It turned out to be a sandstorm that was unlike anything I'd seen before. I kept trying to pierce this ocean of red with my eyes, but felt my eyelids contract with the effort. It was hard to explore the hellish landscape in which we had landed because we couldn't see further than our feet. On top of that, and despite the heat, we were wearing our woollen winter uniform because the aircraft hadn't been fully air-conditioned. Instinctively my hands reached for the thick collar of my jacket and pulled it up over my face to protect it from the sand. For a moment it was as if the whole of Iraq was gathered in the piercing smell of that storm. The smell was familiar, as was the heat of the wind that whipped our faces. The Egyptian Nadia was shaking, and Rula was coughing like she was about to die. I reached over and thumped her back to help her breathe, like I was somehow responsible for what happened to her. This was my country, Rula was my guest, and her wellbeing was my duty.

This movie should be titled *The Delayed Return*. The protagonist returns to the country she left fifteen years before, not as a visitor to her birthplace but as a soldier in the battlefield.

Oh Mary, Holy Virgin, take my hand.

VIII

We were out of the plane. Soldiers came and unloaded it mechanically. We hung about looking for whoever was there to receive us. As far the eye could see, the runway was lined on both sides with boxes—provisions, tools and construction materials. The soldiers untied the bags and threw them on the ground of the airport. We each had to find our sack and pull it aside. Because they were all the same shape and color, I'd written my name with a thick black pen on the cloth. I had two other smaller bags: a backpack and a shoulder bag.

I walked for a distance of no more than thirty yards, carrying two bags and pulling the third. My shoulders felt like they were about to dislocate. As I stopped to catch my breath, I heard Nadia Bayoumi utter the very Egyptian expression, "This night is blacker than sixty tons of tar." I turned to look at her teetering on her high heels and leaning on an African-American soldier who was helping her with her bags. Why wasn't she wearing her boots? She sounded to me like she'd just stepped out of an Egyptian movie, because the only place I used to hear such language was on Arab TV channels. I wasn't certain people actually talked like that in real life.

I drew in a deep breath that filled my lungs with sand and continued my crawl to the airport hall. The glass of the windows was broken and shattered on the marble floor. We heard it splintering under our heavy boots as we walked over it. In every corner of the big hall were American soldiers hugging their helmets and sleeping, lost in dreams that I couldn't begin to imagine. They didn't look like their sleep was broken or disturbed by anxiety or nightmares. They seemed to me, whose back was about to break from pain, as if they were lying in the arms of their lovers after a night of hot sex had sapped their strength. They slept unaware of the tremors that shook the city and of all that awaited them as soon as they opened their eyes tomorrow. Tomorrow was a mysterious word in the glossary of war. It wasn't really a useful label for anything. The sleepers were soldiers who'd arrived here before us. There were others still to come after us.

Baghdad Airport, which used to be called Saddam Airport, was our first stop in the perpetual waiting for transfer to our postings. Each day brought buses and helicopters that would carry the happy sleepers away. There were two soldiers, a man and a woman, sitting on broken benches by a rickety table with a computer and slips of paper, going through the names of the new arrivals and their joining up posts. Being used to playing the ringleader, I led my group towards the registration table and told the soldiers that we were interpreters just arrived from Detroit, so where did we go? The woman said we were to wait for the representative of IntraTrans, the company that was contracting us. His royal highness hadn't arrived yet.

Exhaustion impairs rational thought, and the sight of the

sleepers around us was kind of inspiring. But there weren't enough corners for all of us, and everyone around me started complaining in Arabic and cursing the company and its father. "What kind of mess is this?" "Where the fuck are they?" "They just brought us here and forgot about us?" At some point I pushed my big bag towards the wall, lay down with my back against it, took off my jacket, threw it over my head and slept until morning. Despite the conditions of my impromptu nap, I had a strange dream.

I'm knocking on the door of Grandpa Youssef's house on Rabie Street, wearing a violet wedding dress. Violet isn't really my color, but dreams don't leave us the luxury of choice. My grandfather opens the door, and it's the most natural thing, despite the fact that I know, in the dream, that he's dead. I ask him, "When did you get back?" He replies, "Two days ago. I didn't want to miss your wedding, Sanaa." He gets my name wrong, and I don't correct him. I don't tell him that I'm Zeina, or Zuweina, as he used to call me. But Grandma Rahma appears behind his shoulder and says, "This is Zonzon, don't you recognize her? The little darling got married while you were gone, and here she is returning to us now that she's widowed. My poor child." I cross the garden gate and approach my grandfather, bending over his hand to kiss it. He pulls his hand away and, with that, completely disappears from the scene. At the same instant, the color of my dress turns to black, and I stand there face to face with my grandmother, exchanging looks of sorrow in the cinema-scope of my dream.

IX

Mornings are beautiful even in the devil's house, so how couldn't they be beautiful in Baghdad?

I didn't yawn when I opened my eyes, and I didn't feel thirst or hunger. The sandstorm had passed and the sky was clear. I said to myself that this bright sun was all I needed. But soon restlessness returned and clung to my head like it was part of the lining inside my helmet. I couldn't wait to get to the final destination and take my clothes off and wash the sand and sweat out of my hair. We kept going around in circles, standing up until we were tired, and then sitting back down on our bags. Finally an officer approached us. A handsome young major, although back then I still couldn't identify the different ranks. It was only later that I learned that the leaf that looks like a flower on the chest indicated the rank of major. He yelled, "Anyone here from IntraTrans?" We leaped up and called those missing from our group to join us. They put us on a bus and took us to one of Saddam's palaces near the airport. As soon as we arrived, Nadia Bayoumi started complaining, "Major, I was promised I'd be sent to interpret for our divisions in Kuwait City."

"No," he replied, "your work will only be here in Iraq."

The palace was deserted and in ruins. Broken stones were scattered in the halls, which we crossed like ghosts doomed to eternal perplexity. We ended up in a hall overlooking an artificial lake where, we were told, Saddam used to fish. The garden that was supposed to be a paradise on earth had turned into a swamp full of mosquitoes, a jungle of weeds and grass taller than me. This place had witnessed the end of the world.

We used plastic sheets made from the same material used for refugee tents to set up partitions, dividing the hall into different sections for men and women. Then we were given metal camp beds that we opened and slept on. It was hot and the bugs flying in from the stagnant lake sucked our blood. Still, I was happy to be sleeping in a bed.

In the afternoon the company's representative finally arrived. Where were you, man? He was apologetic as he welcomed us, went over our names and informed us that we'd be staying in the palace for a few days. We were to await instructions with regard to the assigned locations for the different members of the group. Well, there was no rush. All I was really after was a way to send my emails to Calvin and Jason.

I spent the day in the women's section and enjoyed the makeshift shower that would later turn into a fondly remembered luxury. The shower consisted of a curtain behind which you stepped, when your turn came, with a bar of soap and a jug to bathe with water that we filled from a big container. I learned how to pile my dirty clothes under my feet and tread them clean as I showered. Bathing and laundry combined. Soon there'd be no end to my multi-tasking abilities.

That first evening, I had no urge to wander around the palace. Destruction doesn't trigger my curiosity. There was nothing but scattered metal beds on which soldiers slept. I was dressed like them but hadn't yet gotten used to mixing with them. Still, the day ended with a pleasant little surprise. Dinner arrived in bags from the Semiramis Restaurant in the Dawra district. I found out from the young man who brought us the kebabs that it was a restaurant owned by an Assyrian guy. Welcome to the dear cousins!

By the fourth day, we'd all had enough. Finally, the handsome major came with the instructions we'd been waiting for. He said we would all be sent in a military convoy to Tikrit.

"Tikrit? Saddam's city? They must be kidding! Just our luck!"

Of all members of the group, Lebanese Rula and Egyptian Nadia seemed least concerned to learn of our transfer to Tikrit. Neither of them had heard of the city before, and they didn't know what it meant for Iraqis. So while we were all complaining, the two of them remained calm. The major ignored our protests. He knew they were empty. There wasn't a soldier who wouldn't feel special being sent to serve in Tikrit, the city that could raise her children to the highest heaven or cast them underground to the depths of hell.

The major told us to get ready. We gathered our things, which were taken by soldiers, chucked onto two trucks, and covered with a sheet. I climbed into the back of one of the trucks. Three armed soldiers rode with us, and armored vehicles accompanied us, one in front and two behind, a helmet and a machine gun peering out of each.

The hot air stealing in through the gaps in the cover hit our faces and the dust burned our eyes. Still, I wanted to see everything. And what I saw, as we crossed parts of Baghdad, were ruins that I had never seen the likes of before. The burning crumbling buildings through which the wind blew were indeed evocative of the ash that had rained over New York on that painful 11th of September. Pain could only lead to pain, and destruction to equal destruction. Or that was what I thought in my early naive days.

"This is Samarra." An involuntary cry escaped me as the spiral minaret appeared on the horizon. I remembered my personal history in that place. The school trips, the sixth-grade girls with the plaits and white ribbons, the dancing circles to the tune of popular songs under the gaze of Ma Soeur Madeleine, the French nun who was like a surveillance tower watching over us. The egg and mango pickle rolls wrapped in aluminum foil. Was that why those days shone like silver in my memory?

I braced myself against this wave of nostalgia and feigned nonchalance in my smile as I pointed to the minaret and said to those sitting beside me, "I climbed all those steps when I was less than ten years old. All the way to the top." The scenes of my childhood poured over me like hot rain, burning instead of cooling. I watched, as if a feckless tourist, the Bedouin women as they passed by with baskets on their heads, holding the hems of their abayas in front of their faces as they stopped to watch our convoy. The faces were difficult to read, except for the faces of children, who waved to us with thin sunburned arms.

I hadn't given much thought to how Iraqis would receive us. What I'd seen on TV wasn't discouraging. These were people eager for regime change, dreaming of freedom, and welcoming to the arrival of the US Army. Why, then, were the black eyes looking out from behind the abayas overflowing with all that rejection? There was no friendliness in those eyes, or joy. Their irises seemed to be made of the same substance of sadness. What did this country hold for me in the days to come, besides the bones of my ancestors?

I don't remember how many hours it took us to cross what they called "The Highway of Death." We sensed danger whenever the driver suddenly speeded up as we passed through an inhabited town or a major crossing. The convoy didn't stop or slow down for anything until we reached Tikrit. We wound our way into the inner streets until the main American camp appeared before us, a zigzag road and concrete barriers marking its boundaries. Again, the children were waving to us, while the looks of adults surrounded us with suspicion and resentment, looks that seemed to be saying, "Here come the barbarians!" What little energy I had left wouldn't permit me the simple act of jumping out of the dusty truck. My butt had taken a battering from bouncing with every bump in the road, and all my bones ached. In a move of uncharacteristic chivalry, the soldiers helped the women off the truck and carried our things inside.

"Inside" was just another one of Saddam's palaces.

X

Zein. Darling Zayouna. Zuweina. Zonzon. The *zeina*—adornment—of the house. Grandma Rahma always went over the top with nicknames, as if under her tongue there lived a cunning bird that prompted her with words of affection, pampering and coddling. As if she carried, in the deep pockets of her dressing gown, a clockwork device that disassembled the complex letters of any phrase, beating and grinding them, then mixing them anew into delicious little shapes that were somehow easier to digest.

Grandma told me that Tawoos was coming to visit, and I knew that she meant the tall, dark, somewhat masculine woman into whose open arms my brother Yazan and I used to run whenever she came, carrying sesame buns and sweets from her faraway house in Thawra City. Was Tawoos—Um Haydar, as she was known to the outside world—a relative of ours or just a friend of the family? My grandmother gave me a sidelong look, contemptuous of the stupidity that I seemed to have imported from overseas. Could I possibly have forgotten Tawoos, the seamstress, who was tied to us by a lifelong kinship? "All our clothes, all our handkerchiefs and scarves, sheets and pillowcases, come from the work of her hands." That was my grandmother's summarized calling card for the woman who came over every Tuesday to help with her chores, which comprised a list that would've been too long to include in the most up-to-date encyclopaedia: patching up worn curtains; tidying up Rahma's closet; washing and changing pillowcases; ironing sheets and tablecloths; picking oranges from the garden, making juice and filling bottles with it to put in the fridge; making kubba balls and half-cooking them for freezing; preparing the henna mix in the special pan and applying it to Rahma's hair (under the pretext that it prevented headaches); threading Rahma's eyebrows and upper lip; sprinkling cockroach repellent in the corners and drains; washing the yard, sweeping the rooftop and wiping the dust off the satellite dish so that it didn't interfere with reception; burning sandalwood incense in all the rooms of the house; picking olives, seasonally, from the garden, salting them and laying them out on woven trays in the sun; making pastrami by filling the *saandaweylat* with mince and hanging them on a rope in a breeze. The list of chores that this strongly built woman had mastered over decades of being a faithful companion to my grandmother went on and on.

When Tawoos first heard the word *saandaweylat* she thought the women of the house were talking about the hosepipes for washing the rooftop or watering the garden. Or maybe they were talking about sandals, those light shoes that they wore in summer? How was she to know that, in the dialect of Mosul, *saandaweylat* were the intestines of cows, which were filled with a mixture of minced meat, garlic and spices in order to make pastrami? Even after finding out the real meaning, she still found the whole thing too disgusting and kept calling them "sandwilat" instead, with a lighter "s" and shorter vowels, as if by lessening the stress on all the letters she could somehow block out some of the smell. Or maybe she found some similarity with "sandwiches," that other strange word that Tawoos found a bit suspicious.

"I'll tell you a story that happened during one of those long green springs in Mosul. That particular spring was more red than green because of the communist tide. We nearly sacrificed our lives for our *saandaweylat*." I liked it when Rahma expounded her views on politics, sounding like an expert on strategic affairs or CNN commentator when she said things like "communist tide," "American plot," "Zionist conspiracy," "the Jewish Farhud," "Rashid Ali's nationalist movement," "Mosaddegh's coup," "the intrigue of Nuri Pasha" who believed that "the master's house was always safe," "Kissinger's plan," "Nasser's charisma." Even charisma was a familiar concept to Rahma!

"My sister Ghazala telephoned from Basra, a week before Christmas. Apparently I answered in a tired voice and she asked what was wrong, and I said I was exhausted because I'd been mixing five kilos of flour for the festive cookies and had just finished cleaning the *saandaweylat* and preparing them to be *loaded*. That same night security forces knocked on the door and turned the house upside down. When they didn't find anything, they took my two uncles to one of their secret interrogation centers and beat the shit out of them: 'Tell me where it hurts and I'll hit it harder.' They wanted them to confess where the shotguns and machine guns were hidden, those that the women had encoded as *saandaweylat* when they relayed the message over the phone. 'Do you think the revolution is blind to its enemies?'"

I laughed, and my grandmother laughed with me as she told me how the security men came back the following day and headed straight for the fridge. They searched it, scattering tomatoes everywhere and breaking water bottles. Then they screamed at the women: "Where are the *saandaweylat*, bitches?" My uncle's wife, the bravest among them, signaled with her hand towards the red pastrami bundles that were hanging from a rope above their heads, giving off their strong aroma of garlic and spices, and said: "Here they are. You hungry? I can fry some for you and throw in some double-yolk eggs." Tawoos wiped her tears of laughter away and shook the hem of her dishdasha with the inevitable murmur, "Let this laughter bode well for us, dear God."

Grandma Rahma ran a trembling hand over my hair, hoping those stories would win me over to her side. This woman didn't give up easily, and it seemed like her plan was to baste me over a slow fire. She took a little bit out of her pot full of stories and used it to feed the tree of my roots, to bring life into the branches of my belonging. She spread her fingers to rub my forehead, the way she used to drive fear away after a nightmare when I was little. She rubbed vigorously to drive away the evil spirit that had possessed me and returned me to her in a distorted form. "Zuweina, my child, is there any other country on this earth where people entertain themselves with memories of oppression and abuse?"

XI

Calvin had asked me once, "What do you think, Zeina, is the greatest invention of the twentieth century?" In his right hand he had an empty beer can that he was squeezing into a glob of metal. Calvin could consume a chilled beer in two swigs. He would open the can, enjoying the sound of creaking metal, and then he'd take a long first swig made up of multiple gulps, and let out a snake-like sigh, imitating that handsome rugged actor in the Pepsi ad. Calvin too was handsome, at least to me. I once tried to translate for him the Arabic saying about the monkey being as beautiful as a gazelle in his mother's eyes, but he stared at me blankly and said that well, yes, he did actually consider the monkey more beautiful than the gazelle. His realism didn't irritate me. His freedom from the oriental superstitions that filled my pockets and weighed me down, and his lack of a sense of humor, didn't turn me off. Nor did I dislike his ginger curls and the freckles on his nose and his back. I liked Calvin the way he was. If he had been romantic, or gallant, or a bit funnier, with dark flowing hair, I would've been inclined to lose myself in his love and leave the world behind to remain under his feet. The kind of love that borders on obsession scared me. I tried to avoid it so I could stay in control of the rudder of my soul, the only true companion in the days that I often just watched pass me by.

I sat on the balcony and looked at Calvin lying on the bamboo sofa and thought to myself that yes, he was the man for this phase of my life. I was pretty content with the temporariness of what he gave me. Tomorrow, as Scarlett O'Hara had it, was another day. "You tell me first what you think is the greatest invention?" I retorted.

"You really wanna know?"

"Yeah, go ahead."

He got up and went through the door that was held open by a large stone. In one long stride Calvin reached the fridge and returned with the second beer can. One *shabkha* there and one *shabkha* back. That was how we'd describe Calvin's beer-hunt stalk in our dialect. But I didn't have the energy for the process of translating *shabkha* for him. He'd ask me to say it again in Arabic. Then he'd try to pronounce it as if spelling, one syllable at a time, before shaking his head in mock amazement while repeating the word, happy with his linguistic fluency. Finally, he'd take out his little diary and write "*shabkha*" in English letters with the definition next to it.

He continued the conversation, "Don't yell at me, sweetheart, but I think the invention of the century is the remote control."

"Doesn't surprise me at all, you lazy *tanbal*."

I stuck my fingers in my ears as I uttered the Arabic word, to indicate that I wasn't in the mood for explaining what it meant. He nodded obediently, drank half the can in the first

46

swig and let out his usual sigh, before challenging me, "Come on, Zaynaa, your turn. What's the greatest invention of the twentieth century?"

"Ha ha. The nargila, of course."

"But that's a nineteenth century invention, pre-technology."

"Doesn't matter. Lucky for me it stuck around until I found it."

He finished the rest of his beer and sighed happily before commenting on my choice, "I thought you'd choose the laptop." It was true that I never parted with my laptop. But despite our attachment, I didn't appreciate its ultimate necessity until I went to Iraq. If I had to choose between my laptop and the bulletproof vest, I'd take the laptop without blinking an eye. On the white luminous pages of this little machine, on the screen framed by sky-blue, I would record, night after night, my days in this country that seemed to grip me around the throat. For it was there that I launched my own jihad and let my soul go off road, into the dangerous wilderness of wanton abandon.

Was this, my darling, what they call love?

XII

How much curiosity and hunger does the human eye possess? My eyes were two coals blazing from the dust, my eyelids squinted against the inferno of the sun whose power I hazarded at a trillion watts. But instead of hurrying into the shade, I was still intent on surveying my surroundings. We were on a grassy hill, and the dates on the palm trees were dry and shrunken to the size of small grapes. That was where the two trucks had let us off. Twenty-nine new army recruits standing in the grounds of Saddam's palace in Tikrit, our belongings piled up in front of us. A corporal came over with a piece of paper and started calling our names. Whoever heard their name had to take their things and stand aside to wait for the Humvee that would take them to their post. Nobody liked their assignments, and protest filled the air. "But why did you bring us from Baghdad to Tikrit if you're going to send us to Nasiriya or Kut?" Even those assigned to Hilla or Ramadi or Baquba grumbled to themselves as they headed towards the vehicles. Had they been expecting a trip to Hawaii?

A gentle-looking guy called Dawood looked like he was about to be sick. He was being separated from the rest of the group and didn't know where they were taking him. As for the tough guy from Karbala, he stood to one side smoking in silence and throwing mocking looks at the rest of us, poking fun at our petty fears. I later learned the secret behind his bravery. Before emigrating and settling in Philadelphia, he'd served in the Iraqi army. He'd been through both the Iran and Kuwait wars, and the fear in his heart died after having seen more corpses than the rest of us put together. I hadn't heard the word *jeonky* in what felt like a lifetime, but that was what came to mind as I watched that man: an unscrupulous hustler.

We all hoped for a safe assignment. We all hoped for a sip of cold water and a clean bathroom. We hadn't showered in days, and the heat was adding to our grime and stickiness. Was there no end to this journey? And why did we, the five women in our group, have to show more patience and endurance than the men? One of the women with us was about seventy years old. The company hadn't put any age limit on applications. Regardless of your age or religious background or ethnicity or educational level, you qualified for the job as long as you spoke Arabic and English, even if you could barely read them. The corporal told our elder colleague that she would be positioned in Beji. She cried out in panic, "Where is that?" and he answered politely, "Ma'am, they will take you."

Hanaa, who was born in Akra, wanted her work to be there, close to her people. But the list in the corporal's hand took her to Al-Imara. And when Rula was told she would work in Hilla, she said rashly, "I won't go to Hilla. If I'm not placed in the Baghdad Hotel or the Green Zone I'm going back to the United States," to which the corporal replied without

49

hesitation, "Ma'am, we will put you on the first convoy return-ing to Baghdad and you can take the plane from there." Later on I heard that our Lebanese colleague went back and didn't complete her contract. The Egyptian followed soon after.

All the names had been called and mine still hadn't come up on the list. I was still standing after all my travel companions had dispersed.

The corporal approached me and asked, "Are you *Zeina*?"

"Yes sir."

"You're staying in Tikrit. That's why I didn't call your name." So Tikrit was to be my destiny. I returned after fifteen years to find myself in the birthplace of the dictator that we came to overthrow. This was turning into a bit of a horror movie, *No Beast Left in the City*. I got out of the Humvee that dropped me off at my station. The sun was about to set. I stood and took in my surroundings, in a 180-degree pan from left to right. I counted no less than twelve palaces, the biggest being the one I was standing right outside. It was built with some kind of light-colored stone. On every stone of the outer wall were carved the letters S.H. Saddam Hussein. The marble covering the floor was fascinating, with patterns in rose, pistachio-green and violet. I looked up as I entered, taking in the high walls with inlaid wood and the sparkling crystal chandeliers dangling from the ceilings. There was a vast reception hall, still holding some remnants of earlier times, some French-style sofas, Louis XIV and all that. But the upholstery was worn and the wood disintegrating. Did things really fall apart so quickly?

I took the small camera out of my bag and asked someone to take a photo of me sitting on one of the gilded sofas with my leg over the armrest. Vulgarity was necessary under the circumstances. So that was my first photo of the New Iraq.

I wasn't disturbed by the thought of whose backside might have rested on this seat before me, or of how this hall was once crowded with the master of the house and his guests. They were all a bunch of hypocrites and corrupt rulers who'd clung with their teeth to power until the bitter end.

It was a spacious palace, but they couldn't find room for me to sleep on my own. They seemed to have been expecting a male translator. They debated the issue among themselves while I sat on my gold throne awaiting the outcome. I was then taken to a room that stood between the big palace and the guards' house, which was itself another palace, though smaller. My room had once been the kitchen of the smaller palace. I panicked a bit as I looked around me at the boxes of provisions and piles of tin cans that filled the place. But then two soldiers came and carried everything out to be stored somewhere else. I spent the evening washing the floor until the colored marble tiles gleamed once more. Just like that, the guards' kitchen came to be my personal room in Saddam's palace. I opened my big green bag and started arranging my clothes and things into food cupboards and cutlery drawers. The two soldiers returned with an iron bed, sheets and a blanket, and wished me a good night. I slept the sleep of the dead.

XIII

Rahma addressed her morning prayer to the miracle-working silver-framed painting of the Virgin Mary that was placed to the left of her bed. Rahma's style of worship was devised to suit her different moods, her preoccupations, and the state of her health. It was even adaptable to the availability or lack of electricity in that it wouldn't interrupt the soap operas she liked to watch. The morning prayer could be held in the evening, especially when there was a power cut and no TV. There was no harm either in saying her Hail Marys while she rubbed her arthritis-stiff hands with almond oil, or in adding in a massage for her feet, whose big toes curled on top of the others, if she felt like prolonging the prayer. Her ritual was completely her own.

This morning she'd woken up to find there was electricity. So she rushed to the electric massager and proceeded to pray while pressing it in circular movements over her knees. "Virgin Mary, mother of beloved Jesus, preserve what's left of my health and protect me from falling. You are my friend, Maryam, my kind ally and my companion in loneliness. It is to you that I turn in times of trouble and you listen, to you that I pray and you answer, on your door that I knock and you open. I ask you to include our dead in your mercy, O tender one, and to bless my children and my grandchildren and those still living of my loved ones: Kamel and Siham and their children in New Zealand, Jammuli and Sonson and Tamara and the little one whose name I cannot pronounce, Batoul and her husband in America, and their children Yazan and Zeina, the children of my late brother Dawood: Liqaa and Saad in Syria, Samer in Dubai, Youssef, Sabah and Ruwaida in Canada, and bless my sister Ghazala in Jordan and her children and grandchildren in Sweden, London, and I don't know where, and Tawoos Um Haydar and her sons Haydar and Mohaymen and the rest, and our neighbors on the right, and those on the left as far as the third house, and Saleh the gardener. And Mary, don't let the postman Hassoun keep me or the people of the neighborhood waiting. And please remember all those whose names I forgot to mention, but whom you know one by one. Amen.'

The massager froze, and the old woman yelled at the silver-framed icon, "But why, Holy Virgin? Was it beyond your powers to keep the electricity running for five more minutes until I finished the massage?" She searched her memory for the saint in charge of electricity but couldn't remember. She was careful not to disturb the Virgin Mary by knocking on her door for every little thing, so she tried to go directly to the specialist saint for each request. When the children were still at home, they used to make fun of Mama Rahma's way of providing "employment" for the idle saints, keeping them busy so that they wouldn't get bored while sitting on the clouds with their halos around their heads.

Her children would laugh while going over the eclectic group of saints and holy persons that they referred to as the "Cabinet of President Rahma": Saint Anthony was in charge of finding lost things, Saint Rita was the patron saint of emergencies, Bernadette Soubirous specialized in healing the sick, Mar Joseph encouraged the lilies in the garden to grow, and Saint Theresa was the guide to little ways that led to big things. When Rahma started treatment with a physiotherapist, who happened to be Coptic, she expanded her cabinet to include Coptic saints: Saint Cyril, the patron of students during exams, Mar Girgis, who fought evil spirits, Saint Apollonia, who healed toothache and would do for bad joints, and Peter, the patron saint of fishermen and bringer of riches. Rahma remembered Saint Christopher, the patron of travelers, and let a tear escape. "Why do you scatter my family all over your wide world, dear God?" She was missing her emigrant children and unable to forgive the destiny that led her to end up alone in this big house, like she was living beyond her years with no purpose. If fate had had mercy on her, it would have taken her soul at the same moment that her husband Youssef had exhaled his last breath. How right she was to have made it a habit to tell him on any occasion, "God willing, my hour will come before yours, mister." She didn't know then how the wide wooden bed that for fifty-seven years had held both of them would suddenly feel too big for her. During her angry moments, she resented him for leaving her behind, resented the Virgin and the saints who were slow to grant her death wish, and cursed the children who'd flown away without her. She shed the habitual tear, ever and always available, then blew her nose in a small napkin and got up to go to the kitchen.

This morning, Rahma had barely finished wiping away that tear when, minutes after the start of the power cut, the green phone hibernating next to the bed started ringing. Batoul's voice traveled to her all the way from Detroit and brought her incredible news. Was her daughter joking in a moment of good humor or was she lying to her in an attempt to help her cope with her perpetual heartache? Rahma, with the small shrine in her bedroom corner, never doubted that the Virgin Mary would answer her prayers, but for the answer to be so close, practically standing behind the door, this had never happened before. So when Batoul said that her daughter Zeina "had some work" in Iraq and would soon be traveling to Baghdad, the grandmother could not contain her composure and gave praises in her still youthful voice. She looked at the miracle-working picture and shouted, "I kiss your hand, Virgin Maryam, for these good tidings."

XIV

If Colonel Peterson hadn't been an officer with our forces in Iraq, he could've made it in Hollywood. I went in to meet him and receive my assignment on my first morning in Tikrit, and found myself standing in front of a handsome giant in his fifties, with thick eyebrows and a high chin, and a few attractive silver hairs shining through his dark locks. He resembled Burt Lancaster in *From Here to Eternity*. The colonel stood up, shook my hand with his soft plump palm that felt like an airbag, and said, "You got here just in time."

They had one translator and urgently needed a second one, for reasons that I would later understand. A few nights ago they'd raided a palace that belonged to Saddam's wife in which they found countless documents and IDs, and large amounts of money. They wanted to be able to read everything. The colonel took me to an adjacent room, where two tables were covered with sparkling jewellery and ornaments. So these were the kinds of surprises that came with the job. It was like being in a jewellery store in the gold market in Dubai. A pile of papers written in Arabic caught my eye. I leafed through them and came across the Iraqi citizenship certificate belonging to Saddam's wife, with a young photo of her with thick black hair and an upturned nose. Next to the photo was her name, written in blue ink: Sajida Khairallah Talfah.

I felt a cold shiver down my spine as I imagined whose fingers had touched this document before mine. But this wasn't the time for daydreaming. I pulled myself together and told the colonel what the document was. He took it and put it in a folder and wrote something on it. He then led me to the other side of the table and pointed, with his palms opening like a magician performing an amazing trick, to something on the floor and watched for my reaction. Wow! My eyes took in piles and piles of hundred-dollar bills. So many new bundles of money that looked like they'd just been issued by the Federal Reserve. They were ordered tidily in two-foot-high stacks. "Oh my God!" I cried out before I could stop myself. I bent down and was about to pick one up, but pulled my hand back before touching it and looked to the colonel for permission, who nodded encouragingly, "Sure, go ahead." The bundle I held in my hand might have been ten thousand dollars. I wouldn't know because I'd never seen so much money in my life, not even in the biggest casino in Las Vegas. And these were dollars and not gambling chips. "Is this real money?" I asked.

"Of course."

"Aren't you worried that they might get stolen?"

As soon as I'd uttered the question I realized how inappropriate it was, but it was too late to take it back. No, I didn't mean, and it hadn't at all crossed my mind, that one of our soldiers could steal any of the money. If I, for instance, had happened to find a fortune in one of the cupboards of the kitchen where I slept, I wouldn't have taken a cent for myself. I had an experience in a mall in Miami once that I considered a test of character. I'd been browsing through the expensive handbags when I found a bulging wallet on the shelf. At first I thought it was one of the items on display. Then I realized it looked second-hand and that someone must have left it there. I opened the wallet and found fifteen hundred dollars in hundreds and twenties. I didn't attempt to hide it or stick it in my bag and hurry out. I took it, matter-of-factly, to the store security, brought out the ID inside it and asked them to call the woman in front of me. I wanted to make sure that the wallet would be returned to her. Mind you, I'm not stupidly honest. If I was walking down the road and found a hundred-dollar bill on the ground, I wouldn't stop and yell, "Whose money is this?" but would gratefully put it in my pocket and walk on. But seeing six million dollars piled under my feet in a closed room! And in Tikrit, of all places. This was what I'd humbly calla new life experience.

Next to the dollars there were various other bundles of different currencies piled up in no particular order. Iraqi dinars, pounds, and euros. I was told they had been counted, added and multiplied, and found to be the equivalent of three million dollars.

"Look at this." One of the soldiers in charge of the inventory was holding a chain with a big gold heart. I took it from him and opened it. On its right side was a picture of Saddam and on the left a picture of his wife. The inventory was still ongoing, and news of these findings had not yet reached the media.

That was in May 2003.

XV

Her voice was still ringing in my ear since I'd spoken to her on the phone from Tikrit, two days after my arrival in Iraq.

"Zayoun, my life, where are you? Still in Amman? When do you get here, my gorgeous?"

The words stuck in my throat. I stuttered. I didn't know how to break the news to her. Would she be happy or would she start lamenting? "I'm in Tikrit. Don't worry about me. I'm working as an interpreter for a construction company. I'll come visit as soon as I'm given leave to travel to Baghdad."

"What construction in these black days?"

"It's an electricity company, Grandma. They're building new power stations to replace those bombed in the war."

"I can't believe you're actually here, in Iraq. Call me every day, sweetie. Every day, Zein, OK?"

I'd heard that Grandma Rahma was very alert and never missed a thing. She could see through thick yogurt, is what they used to say. I hadn't experienced her abilities firsthand until the second phone call. As soon as she heard my voice, she said sharply, "Listen, Zein, my daughter, I haven't been able to stop thinking since we talked yesterday. I want to come see you in Tikrit. I can't wait any longer."

"But the company doesn't allow visitors."

"I understand. Stop right there. You work with the Americans, don't you?"

She interrupted with the panic of an Arab mother who suspects her unmarried daughter is pregnant and will tarnish the family's honor. The pain in her voice made me fear that her heart would stop beating if I told her the truth. So I lied to my grandmother. I couldn't have done otherwise. I told her I was a UN representative observing the operations of the US Army among Iraqi civilians. I felt life return to her as she listened to me, as if she was eager to reject her own intuitive certainty and believe me, hanging on to the weak thread that I extended to her. She asked in her Mosul accent, which added to the seriousness of the situation, "So who do you get your salary from, daughter? Bush or Kofi Anan?"

I almost replied that it was the same pocket anyway, that appearances didn't make much of a difference. But I reassured her instead, and continued with my fabric of lies, telling her that our role was necessary to prevent American transgressions. I was scared she would demand, like my mother did, that I 'swear on my father's life'. But she didn't. That would've been the only way to catch me out.

Two days later, my grandmother arrived at our base in Tikrit. She introduced herself to the outside interpreter. He sent me a note telling me that Rahma Saour was asking for me at the gate. I changed quickly into civilian clothes and ran outside. She was standing in the line next to the palace wall that was designated for the women who gathered there every day, from early morning, to enquire about a missing husband, register a complaint, or request compensation. I quickly signaled for the interpreter to bring my grandmother to the guardroom. I completely surrendered myself to her embrace and her smell. We hugged and cried while the soldier looked on sympathetically and the Iraqi translator wiped his eyes with the back of his hand. But when I invited her to enter the camp she refused, resolutely shaking her head. It was her Kurdish stubbornness that she carried like a birthmark from the day she was born in Bikhal, and which had been passed on to her daughter Batoul, who in turn passed it on to me. Stubbornness was genetic for the women in our family, like the mule. "I came to this world under the waterfalls," my grandmother took pride in saying, when I was a little girl sitting on her lap, by way of an explanation for her natural steadfastness. She told me the story of my great-grandfather, the pistachio trader who moved between the Kurdish villages and roamed the borders of Turkey and Iran, a determined and stubborn man, whose legacy was passed on by the women of the family, crossing continents, accompanying me all the way to Detroit.

As we hugged, I cried tears of love and nostalgia, and she cried tears of love and frustration, and maybe shame. She must have seen the male and female soldiers coming and going around us, the army vehicles entering through the gate, the interpreters receiving the terrified folk and mediating the rising anger. But things were still unclear during those chaotic first few months. People were still recovering from the earthquake-like shock, still unsure whether to welcome those who'd arrived in tanks or to spit on them.

It was of course out of the question for me to leave the base unguarded, so I stayed with my grandmother in the guardroom, tissues drenched with snot, sweat and tears piling up between us. I was lost for words, so I said, "Is there anything that you need? Do you need money?" She shot me a glance that made my tongue freeze and replied in her wonderfully metaphorical dialect, "*Wallah*, now you can fart from a big ass."

I looked around, embarrassed that any of the translators might've heard her, and my grandmother smiled for the first time since she'd entered the poorly air-conditioned room. She stretched out her swollen legs and smoothed her long dress. She was wearing a pair of new black clogs with thick black stockings, the standard footwear for Iraqi women of her age. She'd arrived from Baghdad in a car driven by a broad-shouldered young man who had long hair, a thick moustache and a deep cleft in the middle of his chin. He was Haydar, she told me, the son of Tawoos. And while I was used to hearing the name Tawoos—Tawoos did this, Tawoos said that, Tawoos cooked this—I still wondered at the strangeness of the name—which meant "peacock" in Arabic—every time I heard it. Tawoos had been with the family since the days before my mother was married. She had dedicated her life to their service and become one of them.

"Have you forgotten Tawoos?" my grandmother asked me as I searched my memory for a face to put to the name. I shook my head and reassured her that I hadn't forgotten. How could I? But I was seeing her son for the first time and had never heard his name. "Haydar. His name is Haydar, Zeina. He's your milk brother." That strange phrase didn't stop me in my tracks at the time. I didn't really take it in. How could he be my brother when I didn't know him and hadn't heard his name before? But the young man was there in front of me, standing next to the car with a bottle of water in his hand and watching me like I was a riddle he was trying to solve. It wasn't until later, when I moved to Baghdad, that Haydar would solve my riddle and I would get used to his presence in my life.

I sat for two hours or longer with my grandmother, talking and exchanging news. She asked about our many relatives who were dispersed in different countries, forgetting the names of children and mixing up the names of cities. Did the Hekmets find asylum in Sweden or in Holland? Who was it who died and was buried in New Zealand, Jalal or his brother Kamal?

She asked about my brother Yazan, and I told her that we called him Jason now, as it was common to Americanize our names. I told her that Yazan had been involved with drugs, but was getting help and hoping to return to school. I talked to her about my mother's illness and her constant cough. "Hasn't she quit smoking?" she asked. "No. She's just as you left her. Smokes excessively and suffocates herself. She has the lungs of a policeman who never refuses a cigarette." My grandmother looked impressed that I still remembered those local figures of speech. She hesitated for a moment before asking about my father. I told her that we didn't see him often since he'd split up with Mom and moved to Arizona. He'd opened a small bookshop there and printed a local classified ads paper. "What happened to the love that your mother took on the world for?" I didn't know how to answer. Although I was pushing thirty, I had never experienced such love that would make one oppose the whole world in order to live it.

My grandmother refused to eat or drink anything at the base. Despite the heat, she pushed my hand away when I offered her a glass of water. As if our water was poisoned. Then she got up and returned from where she'd come. Before the car drove away, I heard her reproof "Was it necessary, this tasteless job of yours?"

XVI

The old woman put her hand on the shoulder of the young man with the thick moustache sitting on the kitchen chair on the other side of the table, and brought her face closer to his. Her paleness contrasted with his darkly tanned skin. Her lips parted to say something but words failed her. Her heart wouldn't let her say out loud what she was thinking. She forced the words, and her voice came out with a strange rattle, like that of a rusty tin can left to the wind. "She's working with the Americans. Zeina's working with them."

"Khala, everyone works with the Americans these days."

"No, Haydar, my sweet. That's not true. None of our relatives or neighbors work with the occupation."

"But she's American herself. She left here when she was a young girl and she became American."

"So Americans forget their roots?"

"No, but Zeina was brought up in a world different from ours."

"We will bring her up from scratch, this ignorant girl.

Right, Haydar, my dear? We won't leave her to her ill manners."
She said the last two words in Turkish for effect: "*tarbiya siz*."

Haydar quickly put his palm to her mouth. "Shush, you shouldn't say that. She's still our daughter." He could not believe that a woman of Rahma's age still preserved, in the folds of her wrinkled skin, all the heritage of generations brought up with a strong sense of justice. His own generation was used to fear and hypocrisy, to bribery and double-dealings, and ulterior motives. They'd wanted all of us Baathists. For those who were too stubborn to join the party, they'd invented the decree that said every good citizen was a Baathist by default. Besides, there'd been an abundance of wealth that had turned their heads. Factories and contracts, schools and scholarships and delegations abroad, hospitals and festivals and magazines and artificial lakes and rivers, tourist resorts and research centers. Then the windmill of war started and drained the oil to the last drop. The men were gone, and the women were left behind beating their chests. Still the winds of righteousness kept blowing between the Tigris and Euphrates, endlessly roaming the land. The breaths of people like Rahma came out under the cover of darkness to blow on the wounds of our souls, to heal the fissures with a secret ointment that was said to be inherited from the days of Babylon and Assyria. So when the Americans came, they found a mysterious country that they couldn't decipher. Their local guides were even more clueless.

"They came riding the occupation tanks." A phrase that was used to describe those local guides. It had a lighter ring than treason. But Zeina was not a traitor in Haydar's eyes. She was a girl who worked in translation and didn't understand politics. Initially he had been happy about this sister who seemed to have descended on him like a gift at a time when gifts were rare. Then, when he opened the shiny wrapper, he felt let down. The present wasn't exactly what he wanted. She was too proud and independent for his liking. She was someone who made her own decisions, made plans and followed them through without expecting help or advice. She was a woman with balls. But as he got to know her, his disappointment was eclipsed by the avenues of conversation that opened up between them. He was elated when she praised his knowledge of music. She was surprised that someone from his conservative neighborhood would know anything of Janet Jackson and the rest of the Royal Family of Pop. He wished he could invite her to his house in Sadr City, to the room that he shared with his brothers, so she could see for herself the biggest collection of Madonna posters in Iraq. Even the ceiling was covered in posters. When it rained, the leaking water sometimes unstuck the glue, letting the pictures fall to cover the sleepers.

How could he possibly take her there? Was he out of his mind? They would make mincemeat of her, grill her on charcoal and eat her fresh off the grill. Al-Jazeera would be reporting the murder of an American soldier in the suburbs of Baghdad. The number had reached three thousand. He couldn't trust anyone, not even Muhaymen, who'd become a different person since he'd returned from captivity. Muhaymen used to collect rare recordings of Billie Holiday and sleep clutching the transistor radio tuned to FM. When they found out he was a prisoner of war in Iran, no one touched his record collection for three years. Tawoos kept them in a box under her bed, and wouldn't sell them even in the direst of circumstances. On his return, he took the box outside, poured gasoline over it and set it on fire in front of everyone. Muhaymen had aged before his time. At forty, he was already an old man.

Haydar had a different mentality. Zeina's choices didn't shock him as they did the old woman. He didn't have anything against the American girl. So he considered Rahma's words and decided he couldn't do what she was asking of him. He said, "Zeina is still one of us. Have you forgotten, Khala, that she drank from my mother's milk?"

"Your mother's milk is pure, my dear Haydar, but the girl has been led astray. Zeina has seen dark days and lost her sense of right and wrong. You must help me."

Haydar shook his head vaguely. He couldn't refuse and couldn't agree. He understood Rahma's heartache, but wasn't enthusiastic about putting his hand in hers to re-educate Zeina. How many thousands of Iraqis, how many millions, did the old woman want to re-educate? No, Zeina could be his only ticket out of the shifting quicksands he was in. She could help him with the immigration documents and take him along to America. There he would catch up on his lost youth, he would drink as he liked, let his hair down, and sing and dance without the self-appointed guardians of virtue coming after him.

Long live America, Land of the Drunk!

XVII

All homecomings are cherished except this one. My arms are open wide to receive all the prodigal children except this girl. Could this really be? Zeina, Zonzon, Zuweina. Her grandparents were inconsolable when she was taken away from them just as she was hovering at the threshold of adolescence. And now she returns, but like this? The girl was herself a beautiful adornment to match her name, and she loved nothing more than staying at her grandfather's house. When she was born, Youssef and Rahma had already crossed over into the land of old age and were just getting used to its pangs of melancholy. Then Zeina descended on them like a bright ray of sunshine, like confetti, as the creative Tawoos used to say. They raised her from the time she was still in diapers, watched over her with prayers and sheltered her under their watchful gaze. Unlike the rest of the family, the child wasn't leaning towards blondness, but had kissable skin the color of roasted almonds. Batoul would arrive in a hurry, leaving her car running as she almost threw the girl on their bed and dashed off to work. With Zeina, the wide bed that was stretched on a solid wooden plank turned into a joyful meadow of play-fulness and laughter. They delighted in her as she grew up and floated around them, answering their calls and serving them like a brunette guardian angel. They hadn't imagined that life would be so cruel as to deprive them of Zayoun. But Batoul could not stay in the country after what had happened to her husband. How could anyone in their right mind believe the allegation that Sabah Behnam, the soft-spoken TV presenter who was scared of his own shadow, had conspired against the ruling party and the revolution?

They had knocked on their door in the neighborhood of Al-Amin at three in the afternoon. Batoul was washing lettuce at the kitchen sink, her husband sitting by the fridge in his pyjama bottoms. When Yazan opened the door, solid hairy arms pushed him aside. Their swearing came in before them. "Where's your pimp of a father? Where's the handsome night-ingale?" Sabah sprang up and in one leap was standing before them. "Yes ... wha ... what is it? Is everything all right?" He received a slap on the face in lieu of a reply. They dragged him away as he tripped over his pyjamas that had slipped down and gathered around his feet. He was gone for just three weeks, but they passed like three eons for Batoul and the rest of the family. If his father-in-law hadn't sought the help of a friend from the old regime, who happened to have a son who was important in the new regime, the poor guy wouldn't have reappeared on the face of the earth. When he returned he was unable to speak, his teeth were broken and he cried nonstop as if they had inserted under his eyelids a reservoir of tears. It was days before he dared to tell his wife what had happened to him. She took him north, to her aunt's house, to get away from the tension in Bahgdad. There, under a pistachio tree in Einkawa, he told her that the denouncement came—by God I swear—from his closest colleague, his crime being that he'd protested about the news bulletins being too long and had said that the news was merely recycled leftovers from the day before.

Before they beat him up, urinated on him, broke his teeth, pulled his tongue with pincers and extinguished their cigarettes on his skin, they had sat him down naked at a table, set up a TV camera in front of him and given him a news report to read. The first item on the report was the execution by hanging of TV presenter Sabah Shamoun Behnam after his having been convicted of conspiring against the party and the revolution. Batoul, who had been brought up in a house where values of truth, justice and dignity were upheld, couldn't let what had happened to her husband pass. She decided to launch an official complaint and went to ask her superior at the university for advice regarding the legalities. "They tortured my husband, Professor!" she told him. The university dean listened to Batoul's complaint, and, being a senior party member himself, laughed embarrassedly and told this staff member who'd come seeking his help, "Tortured him? My dear, that wasn't torture. They were just messing with him." So it was all a game then, when they broke Sabah's teeth, clipped off the tip of his tongue and electrocuted him. The dean himself assured her that real torture would've meant something else completely, something that went beyond a few playful tickles and the dislodging of teeth. If it had been anything more serious, she wouldn't have found a trace left of her husband. In the distinguished dean's opinion, she should thank God for her husband's safe return, smelling of roses and walking on his own two feet.

Batoul left everything she owned, the house, the car and the university job, took Yazan and Zeina and escaped with her husband, one black night, out of the country. A relative forged a passport for the fugitive TV presenter, under the name Korkys Shamoun, occupation spare parts dealer. Sabah grew a heavy moustache and hid his eyes behind thick glasses, to more closely resemble the photo in the new passport. Though he didn't really need the disguise, because no one, seeing the shambles of a ghost that he'd become, would have recognized the formerly handsome presenter.

They arrived in Jordan and submitted their documents to the UNHCR, then waited their turn. Although bribery could have bought the whole of Iraq, Batoul wasn't carrying any testimonies or medical reports or warnings of job dismissal. Sabah's tongue, perforated by a stapler and clipped with pincers, was the only supporting evidence for his family's asylum application.

The grandparents' hearts were broken as they said goodbye to Zayyoun, and they drenched her face with their tears. She was not the first or only member of the family to leave, but she was the sweetest and dearest. And it wasn't going to be a normal trip from which the departed may later return to be reunited with their loved ones, but an escape to a faraway land that felt like death, no later reunion expected or hoped for.

But fifteen years later, Zeina did return.

All homecomings are cherished except this one. It burns the soul.

XVIII

In my black abaya, which covered my body and part of my face, I got out of the taxi that carried me to the old house. The midday sun was as bright as it usually was on winter days in this part of the world. My woolen top was making my neck itch, and I could feel the drops of sweat between my breasts.

It occasionally clouded over. The weather would darken and rain would pour down as if a water tap had suddenly opened in the sky. Then a few minutes later an angel's hand would reach over and turn the tap off. The sky would instantly clear and regain its brilliance, while people down below staggered in the mud and swamps that formed in the twinkling of an eye. The transformation would be so sudden that it looked like it was part of a movie set, with ready-made cinematic props wheeled in from the warehouses of Universal Studios.

I'd been missing my grandmother.

I hadn't seen her since her visit to the base a few months ago now. I'd heard her voice on the phone and talked to her. Her voice was that of an inconsolably lonely woman. She told me about spending a depressing Christmas on her own with the sound of gunshots and mortar shells, talking to the television whenever she had electricity, and waiting to return to God's embrace. Hearing her, I was possessed by a familiar little jinni that I knew couldn't be stopped. Calvin, who'd suffered his share of my extreme moods, used to ask me the name of this jinni and I would tell him it was called Khannas. I laughed as he kept trying and failing to pronounce the "kh" until his throat ached. "From the roof of the mouth, sweetheart. Kha. Kha. Not from the throat."

I celebrated Thanksgiving at the base with my colleagues. They'd brought us all the dishes we craved—turkey, legs of lamb, stuffed chicken and masgoof fish. Everything was cooked by the Bengali and Turkish cooks who'd been contracted by the US Army. They laid out the tables and we lined up, like at school, to fill our plates. We were served by the colonels and generals, as army tradition for Thanksgiving dictated. The ingredients had been brought by trucks from Turkey via Zakho. We knew they'd arrived when packets of pistachios and almonds and strings of figs and dried fruit started appearing on the tables. But could apricot syrup be an adequate compensation for beer? The soldiers were always complaining about the prohibition on alcoholic drinks. On more than one occasion, a local employee had faced punishment when caught smuggling beer onto the base. Some of the army informants would occasionally come to the outer gate with a well-wrapped bottle of Arak and ask for it to be delivered to officer so-and-so. The officer would have paid for it, in advance, in greenbacks.

One day, a woman for whom I'd translated a compensation claim came to the gate with eight big portions of Mosul kubba—a special delicacy of minced lamb and cracked wheat—and left them to be delivered to me. That was the most beautiful present I'd ever received. That evening I held a banquet for my colleagues.

Christmas 2003 followed not long after Thanksgiving, six days before the new year, according to the tradition of Western churches, which celebrated Christmas a few days earlier than Eastern Orthodox ones. One of the army's Christmas traditions was for high-ranking politicians to suddenly descend on us, Santa-like, so that TV cameras could capture images of them spending Christmas with "our sons and daughters in Iraq."

My *Khannas* possessed me when I heard my grandmother's voice on the phone. We were in the first days of 2004, still a few days before Eastern Orthodox Christmas, and my *Khannas* would tolerate no delays. I left Tikrit in the morning, after persuading the commanding officer that I had to go and see a female gynaecologist urgently. He'd told me that that was what the resident doctor was for, but I feigned Arab feminine modesty and insisted that I had to be examined by a woman doctor. I told him that the cleaner, Nahrain, had booked an appointment for me with a doctor acquaintance of hers in Mosul, and that she would see me at her home, not in a hospital. Nahrain arrived at the agreed time and confirmed my story. But the commanding officer was still uncomfortable about my going to Mosul under the circumstances. "What circumstances, sir?" I asked him. "Our patrols are everywhere and I will be back before dinner." Nahrain went out ahead of me. I followed wearing civilian clothes, similar to what city women here wear, and draping the black abaya she'd brought for me over my head. I found her waiting for me on the street with a taxi that a relative of hers drove. I hugged her and thanked her for her help. "I will bear the sin of your lie, Nahrain. I can't thank you enough."

"This wasn't a sin at all. It was a good deed, and God will reward me threefold."

As the car started on the road to Baghdad, I was in a state of disbelief that the officer had permitted me to leave. A recruit of Iraqi origins had been kidnapped and vanished without trace. We heard that he used to visit some relatives of his and had married their daughter. Did one of them denounce him?

We passed devastated buildings and bombed-out areas, followed by fields still awaiting spring to announce their greenness. A few times we passed army convoys, and I was about to raise my hand to salute them but just managed to check myself in time and keep my hand under the abaya, cautious not to meet the driver's eye in the mirror. Finally there were the palm trees marking the outskirts of Baghdad.

As an extra precaution, I got off at the main street then took the first right turn, across from the Tuesday Market. The cold January wind was blowing into me and causing my abaya to billow. A large man wearing a gray dishdasha was walking towards me from the other end of the street. I pulled my abaya across my face, leaving only my right eye exposed to see the road. It's not that I was scared, but watchfulness was a habit I'd developed here. As the man passed next to me, intentionally walking as close to me as he could, I looked him straight in the eye to let him know I was strong and not afraid. I heard him say, "Hey, beautiful. Your eyes can read and write." Good God! I nearly turned back and ran after him and begged him to tell me more of his creative chat-up lines. Where I came from, no one chatted up women in the street so boldly any more, not me anyway. Women here wallowed in the luxurious silk of flirtatious words and smoldering looks which kept their skin and soul protected from indifference and neglect.

How could I ever explain to Calvin, in a short email at that, what it meant to have an eye that could read and write? Would he catch my meaning and, for my sake, oil the wheels of his sluggish imagination as one oils a squeaky door. My poor American lover. No matter what he did, he'd never be able to match that Iraqi drifter who walked past me near the Tuesday Market one afternoon and scrapped the rust off my femininity.

I was stumbling over the hem of my abaya as I searched for the house that, for all the times I'd seen it in my dreams, I imagined I'd be able to find with my eyes closed. But everything in Baghdad had changed. Here I was, finally, in front of the low iron gate, reaching out and ringing the bell but hearing no sound. There must be a power cut, which was good if it meant I'd have the luxury of sitting by the old-style paraffin heater, not that accordion of an electric oil heater, curling myself over it and resting my feet on the smooth metal base, keeping its warmth for myself. It was a scene from a movie I titled *Exquisite Self-Indulgence*.

I crossed the short garden path and knocked once on the wooden door. Before I had time for a second knock, Tawoos opened the door, pulled me inside, closed the door behind me and locked it, turning the key twice and sliding the long wooden bolt into place. She called it *al-saqaata*, returning to me another lost piece from the lexicon of my childhood.

Tawoos couldn't seem to get enough of hugging and kissing me, saying that she too had a share in me. My attention was drawn away from her to the house, which was filled with the aroma of rice, respiring on a low flame—an incomparable scent that masked the damp smell of the old rugs and the weak white smoke of camphor incense. Was it Good Friday or something?

My grandmother walked towards us with effort and pulled me out of Tawoos's embrace and into her own. "I knew you'd come. Blood is thicker than water." She took me by the hand to the sofa by the window, where there was more light, and sat next to me. She started to beat her thighs with her hands like women only do at funerals and catastrophes. The sad look in her eyes as she looked at me said it all. I felt vulnerable and exposed and sat there waiting for the sermon of reproach. I knew what I'd done wrong and had no intention of defending myself. When she'd had her fill of looking at me, she picked up a khaki jacket with gold stars on the shoulders and started polishing its bronze buttons. Every now and then she extended the cotton rag in her hand to Tawoos, who'd place it on the top of a Brasso bottle and, with a deft flip, soak the rag in the heavy liquid. Why were we all sitting in silence?

My grandmother took back the rag from Tawoos and rubbed the stars on the jacket with much patience and tenderness. When she was done, she got up and moved with effort to the closet. She took out a wooden clothes hanger on which a pair of neatly-pressed khaki pants was hanging.. With great care she draped the jacket around the clothes hanger, buttoned it and brought the full army suit and laid it out beside her on the sofa. "Have you forgotten, Zeina? It's the sixth of January. Armed Forces Day." Suddenly the rituals she was performing made sense. She was reliving what her husband used to do every year on this day. For hadn't Grandpa Youssef persisted in marking this day, in his own way, after he'd been kicked out of the army?

I stared at the military uniform laid out before me, looking like a crucifix without a head. Why did my grandmother want to carry this cross for the rest of her days?

I rested my head in her lap and let her tell me her stories that were steeped in the scent of Iraq. She delved deep into her memory for anecdotes and other means of explanation. She told me of my family's history that was manifest everywhere around us: the print of my blood and the bones of my ancestors. I drank her stories in, but they didn't quench my thirst. There was a missing link somewhere, and it wasn't my grandmother's job to find it, but mine.

She said, "They forced your grandfather into early retirement, a few months after the revolution of '58. He didn't belong to the opposition or conspirators or anything. But there'd been an attempted coup in Mosul and they executed those involved and dismissed all the Nationalists from the army."

"But how come Grandpa joined the Nationalists when he was a Chaldean Christian?"

"And why not? Religion never stopped anyone loving their country."

The army had been the dream of every young man in Mosul during the forties. When my grandfather got an army scholarship, and left his hometown to go and study law in Baghdad, his mother cried and considered him an emigrant, although the capital was no further than a night's journey on the train. He graduated and became an officer in the army, moving up the ranks until he earned a colonel's stars. He idolized the khaki uniform, and forced everyone in the house to do the same. Like most men of his generation, he was used to a drop of Arak every evening, but he never touched drink when in uniform. He'd even avoid arguments when he was wearing it, so that if he lost his temper he'd quickly take off his jacket and military shirt before attacking the offender with a tirade of swear words.

Did my grandmother exaggerate her stories a bit, use her imagination to lure me back into the fold? "I swear on the lives of everyone I love that I'm telling you everything as it happened, and the walls of this house are my witness." She told me how Grandpa got angry once, when he came back from his office at the Ministry of Defense to find his younger brother rummaging through his private papers and reading the letters he'd sent to my grandmother from Jenin during the Palestine War in 1948. His army unit had gone to free another Iraqi unit that had been under siege inside the fort of Jenin. They had stayed on for some time after accomplishing the mission. For a while there was a truce, but the war between the Arabs and Jews didn't end. My grandfather snatched the letters from his brother's hand without saying a word and put them back in the drawer. He hurried to the bedroom, took off the army uniform, and reappeared in his underpants to slap my great-uncle.

Colonel Youssef Fatouhy used to take delight in the attention each of his army colleagues paid to his military attire. He told my grandmother that army general Ghazi Al-Daghestany had the most immaculate uniform in the Iraqi army. Unlike that colonel he shared an office with at the ministry before the revolution, who revealed a vest full of holes whenever he took his shirt off during the hot summer months when they were both on night duty. "When that same man was inaugurated as President of the Republic in the sixties, your grandfather thought of sending him a dozen new vests as a gift!"

After my grandfather's retirement, the new leader, Abdel-Karim Qasim, who had been a comrade of his during the Palestine War, sent for him and told him, with characteristic kindness, "Nobody has any doubt about your patriotism or your loyalty to the army. I asked you to join the Free Officers and you refused. However, we did share salt and bread in the past. So I've nominated you for the post of legal consultant to the National Railway. Please don't turn down my offer." My grandfather took the well-paid job and was grateful to the leader. How else would he have supported his large family when he was forced into retirement at the age of forty? Except that legal consultants to the National Railways didn't wear military uniform with shiny stars on their epaulettes. Grandma Rahma sensed his dismay, and so hid the khaki uniform in the storage room. She was worried that seeing the uniform every time he opened the closet would upset him. But on the eve of the first Armed Forces Day after his discharge, he went looking for his uniform and flew into a rage when he found that Grandma had moved it into storage. He removed the mothballs and took the uniform himself to the drycleaner. He returned with it wrapped in glossy white paper, the kind used for wrapping holiday gifts. In the years that followed, family members got used to this sight. When they saw him come home with a white package draped over his arm, they'd say, "Here comes the groom's outfit." They would whisper it, for they knew they'd be in trouble if he heard them. They didn't need a calendar to know that the 6th of January was approaching. If they woke up on a cold morning and found Grandpa polishing the stars on his army jacket, then they knew it was the eve of Armed Forces Day.

With every regime change that followed, my grandfather awaited the phone call inviting him to rejoin the army. But one coup followed another, the years passed and the phone never rang. The hair on Colonel (retired) Youssef Fatouhy's head turned gray, his hearing grew weaker, his army salute no longer shook the ground he walked on. Parkinson's disease affected his legs, and his hesitant steps became like those of a toddler trying to stand up for the first time.

My grandmother was tired of talking. I slipped from her embrace and stood next to the khaki suit. I touched its thick wool with the stark design. It was nothing like the uniform we wore in the army, with its practical camouflage and modern synthetic materials. I picked up the olive-colored beret, ran my hand over it, lifted it carefully, like it was a crown, and placed it on my head. I went to stand in front of the mirror. My grandmother was watching me with tear-filled eyes. Were they tears of anger or affection?

The first time I'd worn a soldier's uniform was at Fort Bliss army base in Texas. Calvin still laughed whenever he remembered how I had come back and told him that wearing the uniform had made me feel masculine. He'd got up from his sprawl on the sofa and given me a half-drunk military salute, spilling some beer from the can he was still holding on his forehead in the process.

But I had been full of pride when they gave me the camouflage uniform. I felt certain I was going on the mission that would finally earn me my American citizenship. It was my chance to repay the country that had embraced me since my adolescence and given me and my family a home. That said, my early days in Detroit hadn't been promising. I was homesick and would cry every night before going to sleep. Every night for three months. Until my mother started to worry about my health and thought about sending me back to Baghdad. But in the fourth month I started school, and my tears eventually dried up. I was drawn into the regular cycle of life. That movie was *Her Return from the Edge of the Abyss*.

I had known nothing about army uniform or military training. When I was first given the helmet I had no idea what a complex thing it was, something that required know-how and practice. Basically it was a bulletproof piece of metal covered in cloth, but it had to be tied in a certain way in order to fit on the wearer's head and settle properly in place. "Remember that a mistake in fitting the helmet could mean the difference between life and death," we were told. The corporal who taught us about the helmet also taught us how to tie the army boots over knee-long socks into which the pants were tucked. As for the army shirt, it was made of heavy material and worn over a brown T-shirt, which made us feel stifled and sweat profusely.

I remembered all that as I weighed the temptation to unbutton my grandfather's jacket and drape it around my skinny shoulders. I was worried that this might upset my grandmother. But she only hesitated a little, then got up and took the jacket with the gold stars in her trembling hands and helped me into it. She was standing behind me so I couldn't see her face. But then she turned me around to button the jacket. She stepped back to look at me from a suitable distance as if contemplating a painting. I could not mistake the meaning of that look in her eyes: what crazy times did we live in, if the dress uniform of an Iraqi colonel could give birth to a bulletproof vest that was made in America?

XIX

I was a Tikriti now!

It was the revenge of my American neighbor whose Lebanese husband owned a grocery store in downtown Detroit. Candice was born and raised in the town of Little Rock before she met Rokuz, fell in love with him, and followed him to Michigan. I used to call her Candice the Tikriti, because she came from the same town as the president, in this case Clinton and not Saddam. Her husband got my joke and laughed at it, while she wasn't sure what I was on about but swore at me jokingly.

I settled in Tikrit as a cultural adviser at the Civilian Affairs Division. An interpreter who not only transferred words between two languages, but also offered the soldiers her sociological expertise. I explained to them, for instance, that entering places of worship was not to be done with shoes on; that they had to give women time to cover their heads before breaking into a house; that people were repulsed by the security dogs as they considered them impure. I told them these things and they were free to take them or leave them.

I was based in one of the presidential palaces. "Like a figment of the imagination," as Rokuz, Candice's husband, used to say when describing to us the wealth of the Gulf sheikhs that he worked with. In the palace I sat on a luxurious chair upholstered in olive-green leather, wide enough for three of me, and wrote at a Napoleon-something style table. At first we used to stop and gasp at every gilded settee or Chinese carpet. We used to go dizzy from looking up at the inlaid Andalusian ceilings and Bohemian chandeliers. But in less than a week we had grown used to the palace and its furnishings, as if we had been born in the arms of such riches. Sometimes we even felt hard-done-by when soldiers in the Green Zone emailed us photos that they'd taken in fancier palaces. They were the children of the capital, while we were the children of the provinces—though the people of Tikrit were anything but provincial. To us, they were more like sophisticated riddles that we couldn't solve.

Men and women came to the gate every day with claims, protests, and demands. Our soldiers had burned down his shop; an army vehicle had run over her cow; the windows of his house had been broken; their whole house had been destroyed by a bomb. We were to blame for every single disaster in this pampered city. I listened and interpreted and filled in forms and gave advice. But I didn't permit myself sympathy or displays of emotion. They came, in the mornings, having stood in long lines before the gate and submitted with resentment to the thorough and harsh search process. We recorded their losses and avoided getting into discussions. A week or two later, financial compensation would be issued, which ranged from a hundred to a thousand dollars. Those were the daytime visitors.

The night's darkness provided the needed cover for other visitors, those who came to volunteer "useful information." That's how they usually described the rumors they passed on, in the hope of a job or a contract or a few greenbacks in return. One of them would come to tell us he knew the location of Ezzat Al-Douri, the King of Clubs in the "most-wanted Iraqi playing cards." "Believe me, he will be in such-and-such a village at such-and-such an hour," he'd say. I'd take down his statement, translate it and pass it to the commanding officer. Another day a young woman with big kohl-lined eyes came to the reception and asked for a private meeting. She wasn't from Tikrit but was studying at the university here. She entered disguised by her abaya and stood in the line for compensation claims. As soon as we entered my office, she threw off her abaya and said that she had "useful information." I took her to a back room and called the intelligence officer and interpreted her words to him. The student said that a group of her colleagues were planning an anti-occupation meeting at such-and-such an hour. She gave us some details then went on about how much she admired the West, how she loved rock music. She was pretty, witty and gregarious, and her English was okay. But I felt uneasy in her presence. I estimated she was less than twenty years old. A fledgling collaborator.

The young informer fell in love with our intelligence officer, Lieutenant Frankie, an African-American from Chicago. He liked her in return and was easy prey for her pointed stares. It got to the point where they were planning to get married. She used to come visit him twice a week. As standard precaution, none of us trusted her completely. For how were we to know that she wasn't planted by the resistance? Even Frankie sometimes had his doubts, and enlisted my help, on the basis that I must know the mentality of women here, to test her out by drawing her into conversation and finding out if she really loved him or if she was pretending. I didn't at all mind being a consultant in matters of the heart. It was like having a part in a movie along the lines of *Juliet in Tikrit*.

Once their relationship reached the stage of holding hands, I left them to it. I didn't really care about what went on between them. I wasn't the vice police. I think he promised to marry her once his service in Iraq came to an end. She believed that he would come back for her and take her to Chicago.

A story that happens in all wars and between all nations. But, the young informant was found, one morning, dead on top of a mound of garbage, with her throat slit and her eyes gouged out. This was the first real shock that put an end to my reckless sense of adventure and placed me near the heart of the tragedy. The first drop of the flood, as my father would say.

At night I had to take part in patrols and in raids on houses where terrorists were suspected to be hiding. Those were long nights full of voices yelling and pleading and wailing, and looks that were sharper than daggers. Strangely what I felt wasn't fear, as much as an awareness that I was going through experiences I had never imagined I'd go through. Yes, there were those who bragged about making history. And we were indeed making a new future for the country that held my ancestral bones and had, once, held me in its arms.

The difficult raids took place after 10 p.m. Our evening in Tikrit started around six, dinner time, the hour when young people in America would be back from work or college and getting ready to go out to the gym or to a bar or a nightclub. Our standard dinner at the camp was shit: dried food in plastic packs. You opened the bag and poured hot water onto the powdery substances, turning them into space-ship dishes of chicken with pasta or meatballs with vegetables. There was also a yellow powder, which turned into something resembling fruit juice when you added water. As a treat, an army cook was sent, twice a week, to prepare hot American meals—sliced ham with mashed potato, for example. I generally preferred the shit bags.

We dealt with our constant hunger by sending one of the local interpreters to a local restaurant once in a while to bring us some roast chicken or tasty kebab. The local interpreters were our envoys to the outside world. They didn't enter the camp but stood at the outer gate to interpret between the guards and members of the public, who were then escorted to the next gate to be handed over to an American interpreter. That would be me.

The first time I scarfed down the local kebab, I hadn't yet built up my immunity and I suffered intense cramps and severe diarrhea. But I didn't give up. I continued to crave the local kebab, which was pure fat with a hint of meat: exactly why it was so tasty. The diarrhea lasted about a week and I lost fifteen pounds.

We had a lieutenant who was six foot five. His name was Benjamin Green and we called him "Big Ben." One day, he came down from his high tower to look upon us, and I was sitting cross-legged on the marble floor of the palace, my sleeves rolled up, before me a spread of kebabs, leeks, spring onions and garlic pickles on an old newspaper. He looked down at me with contempt, like he was a white colonialist talking to a savage native, and said, "What are you putting into your mouth?"

"Kebab."

"How do they allow food in from outside? Couldn't it be poisoned by insurgents?"

"That's why you've got to eat garlic with it. It's strong enough to stop the effect of any poison," I said, extending a clove of garlic pickled in date vinegar to him, the smell of which alone could knock out an elephant. He took it with his fingertips like he was holding a scorpion, cautiously brought it to his nose and suppressed a sneeze. He threw the scorpion back on the newspaper and hurried away on his long legs. I yelled after him, "Don't be scared, Big Ben. It wouldn't explode under your tongue."

Then came salvation. Two women from the northern villages came to the camp looking for work. They'd been cleaners at the Tikrit High School for Girls and had lost their jobs when the schools closed because of the war. Their husbands were disabled Iran War veterans, and they were sole providers for big families. Captain Dixon's heart softened and he decided to employ them as cleaners and to make tea. As I was constantly craving edible food, I studied the women and chose the fatter of the two. "Do you know how to cook dolma?" I asked her in all seriousness, as if it were a security interrogation. She smiled with peasant cunning and answered, "Dolma, biryani, teshrib, everything your heart desires. You name it and I'll bring it." I gave her twenty dollars and asked her for a pot of biryani. She came the following day with a relative helping her carry a pot that was big enough for a whole army unit. That day, I ate my fill, as did Dickson and ten more of the perpetually starving soldiers. It was a meal the likes of which they'd never even imagined. From that day on, Nahrain became my personal cook. She also started taking my clothes to wash and iron in return for a few dollars.

We ate by day, and by night, as the city slept and anxiety and fear abated, we raided. I went out on my first night raid ten days after my arrival in Tikrit. They called me to accompany the unit raiding a house in which we were told Al-Douri was hiding. We didn't come across him there. We found an underground tunnel that led to a vehicle of the type that's attached to the back of pick up trucks, big as a mobile home. We later found out that he'd left before we arrived. We always arrived after they'd left. An Iraqi-produced version of *The Fugitive*.

XX

The author opens her desk drawer and brings out a bundle of newspaper cuttings and human rights reports that she tosses in my direction. "Read these," she says.

I know what's in them. Every night I sit cross-legged on my bed, place the laptop in front of me and criss-cross continents. I read about false intelligence and cooked up reports, about resignations from the president's advisors, about the president's slips of the tongue, about his lies, about controversies between the Pentagon and the CIA. I read about protests in America, about numbers in the billions. I read online and see with my own two eyes what the screen cannot show. I watch army coffins being shipped home. Friendly fire; Al-Qaeda; Zarqawi; corruption; systematic plundering; sectarianism; mass exodus. Reporters murdered. Iraqi scientists murdered. University professors. Men and women.

"Yes. What do you need me for now? You have piles of documents to help you finish the novel."

"It's not me who's writing. It's Rahma. Haven't you figured

that out yet?"

Has my grandmother put her up to this? What use is it to Rahma if she manages to ply my head open and fill it with all her own values and life experiences? My grandmother was as mad as Tawoos. Just a different kind of madness. Tawoos once told me, "When I die, don't bury my hands with me."

I winked at my childhood nanny and said, "Have you heard of an afreet dying?"

"We all die in the end. And I don't want these hands to be eaten by worms. So when I stop breathing, take my hands and wear them over yours, like gloves." Tawoos opened her palms between us and mourned her manual skills that would be buried with her. "Have you ever seen hands like mine, Zeina? Skilled in so many things? They can cook and mix dough, embroider and sew and sweep the floor and wash clothes and beat rugs; they can iron and plant and harvest and milk the cows and pluck chickens and feed birds; they can saw wood, bandage wounds, hammer nails and give the finger. What more do you want?"

Just as Tawoos wants me to inherit her hands, my grandmother wants me to inherit her memory. And the author likes that because it serves her novel. She's good at nothing but writing, the only work that defies Tawoos's capable hands. It was noble work, in people's eyes. Unlike sweeping and polishing. But it's also work that has the power to bend the truth.

Every time I try to escape her, I see her shadow behind me, attached to my own. The two merge until I can't tell them apart.

Even my grandmother fears what the author is doing. She doesn't want the words taken out of her mouth and confined to paper. Paper is incapable of conveying the hoarseness in her voice or the heat of her breath. What my grandmother is after is a direct channel from her memory into my consciousness, without the author's mediation. That's all she lives for now. I don't know what gave her the idea that my family history would redeem me. That she can use it to put me back on the righteous path and to correct the directions of my compass. The stories she tells me mirror the history of the homeland. Her characters are perfumed with the scent of Iraq, and her education program takes no shortcuts. It's full of committed employees, loyal craftsmen, and teachers who dedicated their lives to the blackboard, integrity being the real protagonist. Wasn't there a single person in the whole family who was idle or corrupt? Could a movie be suspenseful without villains?

Let me be the villain then! I would be the element of suspense, the conflict that made any drama possible, the hook that holds the author's interest in the story. I don't know how far she is in the novel that she's stealing from my life. Does she still hate me? Does she still take Rahma's side, and portray me as the traitor and my grandmother as the epitome of authenticity? How did she know Rahma wouldn't slip from between her keyboard-hitting fingers and go to meet her God, anyway?

So Rahma might die. And the author would kill me off too in the end. She would arrange abduction, or a mortar, or a roadside bomb under an army vehicle. If I had the choice, I would go for friendly fire. With my own hand, not my enemies'. I don't feel like satisfying the blood thirst of any Mujahideen. I know she wants to have a black bag placed over my head, have me shot at close range. That's how treason is supposed to be punished. But I refuse to die a coward's death. I demand the chance to fight back.

Come back here, don't go. Restart the computer. Don't interrupt.

XXI

We were told that he was an evil bastard.

He was a security official in the former regime. It was people like him that we were supposed to be holding to account for their crimes against humanity. There was no pity for someone like him. As long as he, and others like him, was free, Iraq could not rise up and give its rendition of the hymn of democracy. It was midnight when we headed in three vehicles to the house of that contemptible man. Twenty soldiers got out and surrounded the house. They were armed to the teeth, but to me they looked like panthers moving in the dark. I waited in the Humvee with two soldiers guarding me. I wasn't scared but I was nervous. It was my first real raid.

Four of the soldiers broke the iron garden gate, went into the yard, kicked the wooden door and were inside. Inside, a family was sleeping; a woman woke up and started screaming. Then a man appeared in his white dishdasha, holding out his open hands towards the soldiers and saying "Yes … Yes." They shouted and gestured at him to lie face down on the floor, and he immediately understood. He dropped down quickly as if he'd been trained for situations like this. They ordered him to extend his arms to the sides and he did so. A soldier stepped forward and tied the man's hands behind his back with a nylon wire. Then they called me over from the vehicle to do the interpreting.

I looked at the "target" and the M16 aimed at his head, and I noted his good looks: green eyes and a tall figure whose dignity was emphasized by the white dishdasha. Not many people could continue to look dignified while lying face down on the floor.

The unit's sergeant brought out a piece of paper from his pocket and told me to ask the man his name.

"What's your name?"

"Mohammad Khalil."

"Your full name."

"Mohammad Khalil Mohammad Ayash Al-Abeedy."

He sounded as if he was choking on his pride. From an inner room we heard children crying. The name that the "target" had just given didn't match the one written down on the sergeant's piece of paper. From the open door a woman appeared with uncovered hair and a light-colored dishdasha. She addressed me directly, her voice full of panic, "Sister. Wallah, my husband's done nothing. He's done nothing, wallah."

My lips trembled and I struggled to keep my composure. On my own initiative, and without double-checking with the sergeant, I reached out and gently pushed aside the weapon that was aimed at her husband's head. I said, "It's nothing to be scared of. Just a simple investigation."

The sergeant was asking me, "It this the man we want?"

"Not according to his name."

He told me to ask him for ID.

"Where's your ID?"

He'd barely lifted his head towards his wife when the sergeant shouted and aimed the weapon back towards the man's skull. "Face down on the ground!"

The "target" did not need my interpretation to understand what was required of him. He swiftly stuck his cheek to the bare yellow and black tiles. I intervened again and whispered to the sergeant, "Take it easy. He's asking his wife to bring his ID."

I received a look of gratitude from the green eyes before they returned to the floor. The man said to his wife, "Quick, bring the ID quickly, from the drawer under the TV."

The woman went looking for the ID but couldn't find it. She was panicking and confused, yelling from next door, "I can't find it! Where the hell is it? Where did you put it?"

I interpreted what she was saying for the sergeant, while the man on the floor was grinding his teeth as he yelled back to his wife, "Check the closet by the TV, woman!"

A few moments later, the wife returned with the ID. I read it and handed it to the sergeant, pointing to the name that didn't match the paper at all. Neither the first name or the father's name, nor the grandfather's or the family last name. Under profession, it said "teacher." Again I confirmed to my colleague that this was not the wanted man. The sergeant, who had three sharp-angled lines on his arm, relaxed and ordered the soldier to cut the hand ties. They helped the man up and sat him on a chair, before the sergeant asked him one more time for his full name to confirm that he was the owner of the ID. The man repeated the name. I directed my colleague's attention to the fact that the man was a teacher, so he asked him about his profession. The man replied, "I am a professor at the University of Tikrit."

The sergeant asked him if he knew so-and-so—the man whose name was on the piece of paper—and he answered, in English, "No."

"Oh, you speak English?"

"Yes, I do."

But then the man seized this moment of calm to address me in Arabic, "Sister, please, explain to them that I'm not from this city and don't know anyone here. This is my first academic year at the university."

The sergeant stepped forward, bowed before the man, shook his hand and said in a theatrical tone, "Sir, please accept my apology."

The man of the house, whose door we'd broken fifteen minutes before, replied, "No problem, it's okay." He repeated it a few times, his eyes watering in disbelief at the fact that he'd survived. I too could not believe it. I was finding the scene before me very moving.

We gave the man a compensation claim form and left through the broken door. But we didn't return to the base right away. That night, we went and broke the outer gate of the neighboring house. Then we knocked on the inner door and a stooped old man came out, also wearing a white dishdasha and carrying an inhaler, and behind him stood a woman of the same age. There was no one but them in the house. After examining the ID, we confirmed he was not the "target" either. We apologized and gave him a form for the cost of the outer gate before leaving to break someone else's door. But before our soldiers aimed their boots to kick the third door in, we heard the sound of a car speeding through the parallel street. The curfew had started at 9 p.m. and not even a fly would dare move at this hour. We dropped everything and ran back to the vehicles to chase after the fleeing car, but we only caught up with it when it stopped outside Emergency at Tikrit Hospital. The driver was helping an old man out of the car and supporting him through the hospital doors. We followed them inside and confirmed that the old man had suffered a heart attack and needed urgent treatment. We examined their IDs and the name of that son of a bitch we were after wasn't among them.

So we returned to the base a little before dawn, and I didn't sleep that night. When I got up for work a few hours later, I was still carrying a mental image of the university teacher with his cheek pressed to the floor, and his attempts to hide his humiliation in front of his wife and children, and even worse, asking us to excuse him. That image would be responsible for many nights of insomnia to come.

The three months I stayed in Tikrit were depressing on more than one account. The summer heat was unbearable. On nights when I slept on the terrace to get some air (the air-conditioning was broken), I was tormented by the mosquitoes, and the tanks and Humvees that passed by my head on their way to the raids. To add insult to injury, there was no bathroom where I slept, whether with hot or cold water. What a miserable life for a palace!

I was deprived of the basic God-given right of having a toilet nearby. "Use a plastic bag," was the advice I received from one of the kitchen workers. I used to follow it when desperate. Other times I would walk to the other palace and jostle in line with the soldiers for their restrooms, which were like high school toilets: filthy and with obscene graffiti on the walls. There was always someone standing outside and peeking through the cracks or pestering you with questions or protesting that your shit was taking too long to come out.

For all these hardships, I let out a scream of savage delight when I was told that I'd be leaving Tikrit and transferring to the Green Zone in Baghdad.

XXII

"What do you say we raid her house?" said Donovan, my new captain in the Green Zone, one hot July evening. I thought he was joking.

In July, water boils in the jug, as the Baghdadi saying goes. That's why we were sitting on the edge of the artificial lake with our feet in the water. The lake was no longer fit for swimming now that weeds had started growing in it and green-blue spots were floating on its stagnant surface. The soldiers who'd arrived here at the beginning of the war told us that the palaces were like something out of *A Thousand and One Nights*. There used to be an army of horticulturalists whose job it was to cultivate and maintain the garden, and they'd brought rare flowers and plants from all over the world. The lakes used to be as clear as glass, wild geese and river fish roamed in them. Then the new government officials and the members of the new ruling council arrived with their guards and wreaked havoc in the place. Gone were the specialists in roses and jasmine. The water fowl were barbecued.

At first I didn't get Captain Donovan's drift. I was asking him about the possibility of visiting my grandmother, whose house was just half an hour away by car from the Zone. So he suggested we raid her house, and it turned out he meant what he said. He didn't oppose the visit but worried about drawing the neighbors' attention, and so implicating my grandmother and putting her in danger. He argued she'd become an easy target for terrorists if anyone suspected that her granddaughter worked with the Americans. "So what are you saying?" I asked.

"If you want to see her, there's only one way: we can raid two or three houses on the street. Her house will be one of them, and it'll look like a normal search patrol."

At dinner that same evening we discussed the plan with the rest of the unit. We would run investigations in the neighborhood, under the pretext of looking for suspects, then we'd raid her house. A raid usually takes over two hours. So I'd have plenty of time to get my fill of my grandmother, while the soldiers rested on the sofas of the lounge, ate watermelon and looked at the icons of saints. We had our plan, set the date, and carried on drinking Coke and devouring glasses of jelly in an attempt to cool down. The more we ate and drank, the more we sweated.

It's time for me to step away from the keyboard and into the scene. I want to live this visit outside the text, play my true part which lies beyond arranging words. So I'll let the author describe, in her high style, what happened during that pretend raid. She's visibly relieved at my withdrawal and starts to write:

The turquoise ceramic piece still hangs in its usual place at the entrance of the house, warding off evil with its seven eyes. The smell of the oil lamp welcomes the arrivals and announces yet another power cut. The darkness of the night and the noise of the approaching armored vehicles have turned the neighborhood streets into a ghost town. The same darkness is a convenient cover for Zeina and her friends. One of the soldiers knocks heavily on the door, and it's opened by Rahma herself. Three soldiers go in first, followed by Zeina, who quickly closes the door behind her and, despite the darkness that is broken by nothing but a lonely candle, rushes to make sure the curtains are also drawn. The rest of the unit stay behind, in the safety of their armored vehicles.

At the heart of the living room, a big picture of the grandfather hangs in the middle of the wall. A beautiful old picture, with him in his military uniform and his colonel's stars. But because Zeina only knew her grandfather with white hair and a receding hairline, she thinks that the picture is of her youngest uncle, until she picks up the lantern and moves closer. The grandmother has been prepared for the raid. Her American granddaughter explained the plan to her on the phone. She objected at first, couldn't see what interpreters would have to do with the search operations of the occupation. Zeina replied that monitoring raids was an integral part of her job. Rahma's longing to see her beloved Zayyoun blinded her into believing and accepting. But despite all the preparation and anticipation, the old woman screams and slaps her own cheeks the minute she sees her granddaughter in the distinctive light-colored camouflage of the US Army. She doesn't recognize her right away, not until Zeina has removed the helmet from her head. And Rahma still wishes that the woman standing before her was only wearing these clothes as disguise, that she'd only borrowed the helmet to protect her head from the stray bullets that fill the Baghdad air. But she knows that her eyes are only confirming what her heart has been telling her for some time.

God damn you, Zeina, daughter of Batoul ... I wish I had died before seeing you like this.

The granddaughter squirms with embarrassment in front of her comrades, but none of them understand what the old woman is saying anyway. She goes up to her grandmother to embrace her, but Rahma pushes her away and goes inside. Zeina follows her to the bedroom, that large rectangular space that's filled with memories and laughter, the echoes of family arguments, the prayers and lullabies of the past. Rahma has collapsed on the old low chair with the wide wooden armrests. With heavy eyelids she looks at the soldier standing in the doorway and wishes again that her eyes were deceiving her. She wishes she'd go blind, or the girl would point to something behind the curtain and say, "Smile, you're on *Candid Camera.*" But it isn't *Candid Camera.* She knows it's not. And Zeina isn't removing her disguise. She just closes the door behind her and becomes a ghost moving in the darkness of the room. She throws herself into her grandmother's arms. Clings to her. Persists in holding her close. Even as the old woman resists the embrace like a sulking child. Zeina holds on to her grandmother and rocks her back and forth. She starts singing ...

Dil dil dilani
To Baashika and Bahzani
Baba went to old town stall
Brought us chickpeas and raisins ...

The girl steals her grandmother's lullaby. Out of the same memory well, she pulls the words, the tune and the rhythmic movement and claims them for herself. Two women in a familiar portrait, places reversed. Rahma fights with the little strength left in her, but soon surrenders to the hands that caress her head and face and wipe the tears from her wrinkles.

"Shame on you, Zayyoun. You're lost, my child. My heart is broken over you."

"Grandma, listen to me, don't take it like this."

"And how do you want me to take it?"

"We're doing a good job in this country. Believe me."

The old woman pulls her head away and looks contemptuously at her granddaughter.

"Don't you dare say these things in the room where your grandfather's soul ascended. Have some respect for his memory at least."

"He died here?"

"Here on this bed. It was a mercy from God that he died before witnessing the occupation, before witnessing you."

Zeina can't see the old woman's tears in the dark, but she could smell them. She can see her grandmother's voice, and it's pale and trembling.

"Here on the same bed, where you used to play as a child. When they took you away from us, it made us ill and old. Your grandfather and I felt like orphans."

"Why do you cry now, when I'm here with you?"

"If only they'd known how to raise you properly when they took you away, my daughter's daughter."

"I'm the way you made me. I haven't changed."

"You have changed. You belong to the Green Zone now."

Zeina continues to wipe the tears away from the tired face.

She passes a hand over the bedspread that's weighed down by the heat of the room. That pillow over there, by the window, that's where her grandfather used to lean while reading the newspaper. She can only remember him with his glasses and the newspaper. He read aloud and made sarcastic comments about the news. His voice lives on in the room. Her grandmother would listen to his comments, put her finger to her lips and whisper in real fear, "Shh ... you'll get us all into trouble, man!"

Zeina looks over to the far corner of the room where a candle burns before a picture of Mary, the mother of miracles. The candle flame has been flickering since she left it fifteen years ago. The picture is settled in its place on the small table, propped against the wall, with the same white crocheted table-cloth under it. But something is missing. Where's the gold that was sacrificed on the Virgin's altar? The jewelry that used to adorn the frame is gone. Nothing sparkles in the picture. Zeina gets up and moves closer, to be sure. She asks her grandmother, "Has someone stolen the Virgin's gold?"

"No. I sold it."

"Grandma! You sold the Virgin's gold?"

Life returns to the old woman's voice. "Did the Virgin, bless her name, need the gold when we were suffering under the sanctions? I sold it to pay for Tawoos's dentures."

The returning granddaughter suddenly remembers that dark years have passed here. She's heard how families sold their furniture and sat on the floor, how even the wood of the doors and the iron of the window frames were sold. But those days are gone now. She looks tenderly at her grandmother, as if to say, "Don't worry. We've come and we've brought salvation." But the old woman, who sees the hidden glow of eyes in the dark, who reads minds like the fortune-tellers of Babylon, shakes her head and murmurs, "The worst is yet to come. We can only ask for God's protection."

On the wall above the bed Zeina sees a white crucifix adorned with seashells and framed on a red velvet background. The room is more like a chapel than a place to sleep. Above the crucifix an empty black nail sticks out from the wall, with a faded rectangle where a picture must've been recently removed. "Whose picture was it that used to hang here?" Zeina asks. Rahma looks to where Zeina's pointing. That girl doesn't miss a thing.

"Tawoos came one day and said that Saddam was visiting people in their homes. He just knocked on the door and walked in like fate with his bodyguards. He wandered through the rooms, lifting the lids off cooking pots to see what ordinary people were eating. She said it was best we get a picture of him and hang it somewhere prominent. Your grandfather refused at first, but we argued over it until he reluctantly gave in. Haydar got us a framed picture for a few hundred dinars. He said it was best to put it here, to ward off evil. We placed it above the cross. But he never came. And after the war we took it down."

As night descends, the rooms of the big house feel more desolate than ever. Zeina worries about her grandmother. "Aren't you afraid of the lack of security in the city, Grandma?"

"Who would I be afraid of? Tawoos comes to me every day, and the people of the street have known me for forty years. As for those new militant riffraff, they don't bother me. Muhaymen has told his group to look out for me."

"Who?"

"Muhaymen, Tawoos's third son. Haydar's brother. He was a prisoner of war in Iran. Now he's with the Mahdi Army."

It's no longer just the lack of light in the room. A dark mist has veiled Zeina's eyes, and fever rises in her cheeks. What would Captain Donovan do if he found out that his favorite interpreter had a brother in the Mahdi Army?

XXIII

I didn't repeat that visit to my grandmother in her home. As she hugged me at the door and choked on her tears, she said that she'd break my legs if I ever came back with "those lowlifes." She threw me out, crying and thanking God that my grandfather's eyes were closed forever before seeing "the shame" that his American granddaughter had brought upon them.

Back at the Zone, the place that defined me now, I found a commotion at the checkpoint and raised female voices. There were three veiled women from the parliament, protesting at our dogs sniffing their clothes. I didn't want to get involved in interpreting and slipped quietly away. What the hell was going on here?

I found Shawn, Hamilton, and Bill doing what looked like a sketch in the middle of a laughing crowd of male and female soldiers. Army soldiers would do anything to combat boredom, including waking up volcanoes and bringing meteors down from the sky. One of the boys was holding a baseball bat and aiming it vertically at his forehead. Another was making wailing noises and raising his right hand and bringing it down on his chest in a steady rhythm. The third was jumping up and down and repeating "Hey da. Hey da."

I didn't get it right away. But when I was told that they'd just come back from a patrol in Kadhimiyah, where they'd seen the rituals of Ashura, I understood that Bill was supposed to be saying "Haydar." He pronounced it as he heard it and didn't know that it was one of the names of the Shia Imam. I didn't know what got into me. A joke is just a joke, at the end of the day. They were tired, and the summer was hot, and a little distraction couldn't hurt anyone. But their laughter irked me, even though the religion they were mocking wasn't my own. Let's say that I'd just grown up to the sound of its muezzins. So I acted like any religious fundamentalist.

"OK, Shawn. Let's do the sketch of worshippers by the Wailing Wall. You know the ones who move their heads back and forth like clockwork toys." It wasn't even my voice coming from my lips. It might've been the voice of my father, the TV presenter, or maybe the voice of Tawoos, or my writer alter ego who'd learned to imitate the pitch of my tone…

Everybody looked at me in astonishment. As if I'd just spilled a bucket of water over somebody's head. The sketch ended and the laughter faded away. Hamilton came over and put a hand on my shoulder, "We were just kidding around. Whose side are you on anyway?"

"Not the side of morons."

"Let me buy you a coffee."

We went to the canteen and sat at a table where some newly arrived recruits were sitting. Hamilton went and stood in line. I was absent-minded. I remembered my Aunt Jawza.

One day she crawled across Jumhuriyya Street on all fours. Her son had polio and she vowed to crawl from Khellany Square to the Miskanta Church near Midan Place, in the hope that the Virgin would take pity on her and heal her only son. When she got there, the skin on her legs was peeling off, but she was optimistic as she abandoned herself to the hands of Manoush, the old churchwarden, to complete the ritual. Manoush was a short, fat old woman, who carried the tools of her trade with her at all times: a thick metal chain with a hook and catch at the end.

A woman would come to Manoush praying and weeping, overcome with emotion and fear. Manoush would try to calm her down as she fastened the chain around her neck and locked it, the audible sibilants of her murmured prayers mingling with the woman's sighs and the ringing of the church bells. Then Manoush would attempt to take the chain off with one swift movement. If it resisted, it was a bad omen, and the chained woman left pale and distraught. But that day the chain around my aunt's neck slipped off right away. She cried tears of gratitude and thanked God, who cared to look upon her distress and include her in His mercy. Manoush pushed her chest towards my aunt for a handful of dinars to be placed into her cleavage.

Whose side was I on?

Hamilton returned with the coffee and knocked on the table to wake me up. I told him my aunt's story. Others at the table listened too, and thought my Aunt Jawza's story was "incredible," "fantastic," as if I was telling it for their entertainment. The only one who understood was Manuel, the dark-haired soldier of Peruvian origins that Deborah had a crush on. He was jumping up and down in his seat as if I were telling a story that he was only too familiar with. Then he told us about the

Good Friday procession that took place in the poor neighborhood where he grew up in Lima. Every single time, the priest selected José the postman to play Jesus as they re-enacted the crucifixion.

"What? Because his name José means Jesus?" someone asked.

"No, not that. Half the town was called José. But because he was the only one who had blue eyes."

They took the post bag off José's shoulder and appointed him their personal Jesus for the day. On Good Friday, the deacons lifted him onto the cross, punched holes through his palms with the nails and mercilessly pushed the crown of thorns down on his forehead. He bit his lip obediently and suppressed his cries of pain. Crying was for children, not prophets. After the ceremony was over, they spent the whole year treating his wounds, and by the time they'd healed he was ready for another crucifixion the following Easter.

"Manuel, are you on the deacons' side or on José's?" I asked.

"José's."

"And I'm on my aunt's side, who returned from that church with bleeding legs and peace of mind."

When the order came for me to transfer to Mosul, phone calls between my grandmother and me became few and far between. Terrorists were getting more active in the cities, and more interpreters were needed everywhere. Arrests were being made by the thousand, and they needed us at interrogations. It was hard work, but the general mood was actually calmer than in the capital. In Baghdad, the city itself was burning, although the Zone remained safe. "The master's house is always safe," as Nuri Al-Said had believed. As we too believed for as long as we lived within its walls.

In Mosul my life changed. Public relations entered it, and social expectations. I got to know a few young women from the neighboring villages. University graduates who were on the lookout for husbands. Who dreamed of going to America and getting married there. "Amreeka" they pronounced it. They imagined all the men there were millionaires. I also met other interpreters who worked for the Marines. One of them was a young man from Basra who'd lived in Boston and spoke English with the accent of a British lord.

"Where did you learn such birdsong, Malek?" I asked.

"In Oxford."

Malek had a PhD in Comparative Literature from Oxford University. His thesis was on the use of myth in Shakespeare's plays and Sayyab's poetry. Why had this singing nightingale left the fine silver of literary tropes and opted instead for the cheap tin of security interrogations?

We became friends. He used to call me Zen Zeina, and I called him Sad Malek, which was the Arabic name for a type of heron that lived in Iraq and was said to sing beautifully when injured. Malek suffered from boredom and chronic depression, and we had long talks about how bad things were getting in Iraq. He ended every discussion on the same note: "We ate shit, Zeina my dear." Even Shakespearean eloquence was corrupted by the army.

My closest friend, however, was still the laptop. I wrote my emails to Calvin on it, and received an outpour of bitter political jokes every day. Iraq became a joke factory. There were jokes about the Kurds, about people from Deleimi, Mosul and Nasiriya, about the potheads. Every sect had its skilled jokers who specialized in mocking the other sects. There were also jokes featuring the president and the politicians who came to power on our coattails. Everyone was equal in the eye of the joke. That seemed to be the only democracy we had brought.

I found Sad Malek to read him the latest of my online finds: a list of the most used words and phrases in Iraqi conversations since the start of the war. It was supposed to be a joke, but Oxford Boy listened to me with a grave look on his face.

"Generator. Power cut. Water shortage. Traffic jam. Car bomb. Thief. Twenty liters water quota. Ration. Raid. Dead. Kidnapped. Escaped. Assassinated. Iran. Constitution. Petrol. Collaborator. Diesel. Explosion. RIP. ID. Mortar. Bremer. Americans. Stoned. No signal. Federalism. Farewell."

"Didn't I tell you that we ate shit, Zeina dear?"

XXIV

Grandma arrived in Amman on a snowy day in February. I stood on the sidewalk waiting for the car. She was lying on the back seat, and at first I thought the driver was Haydar. But when I drew closer to greet them, I realized that he looked like Haydar but was older.

It was before five in the afternoon, but an early dusk had already descended on the snow, turning its white into a luminous blue. In that magical light I watched him get out of the car after hours on the road and stretch his slender figure. He opened the back door and took my grandmother's hand to help her out. With his soft beard and a yellow scarf wrapped around his neck, he looked a bit like a medieval monk to me. Muhaymen, my other so-called brother, carried my grandmother's suitcase upstairs to the place I was renting in Deir Ghbar. It was quieter here than Shumaysany and Suwaifeya, not as crowded with other Iraqis. For the neighbors, I was one of many Iraqi exiles for whom Jordan had become a place for the scattered families to meet, a safe sky for the migrant birds of

Iraq. For Muhaymen, I was just Batoul's daughter, and Batoul was Rahma's daughter. Rahma was sick and needed surgery, so her granddaughter had come all the way from Detroit to take care of her. It was the story that my grandmother and Haydar agreed on. Did they need to protect me from Muhaymen?

I didn't even know Haydar well enough to trust him, but my grandmother thought of him as her own son. She confided everything in him and included him in her plans. And I had tired of scheming, of negotiating my way around endless security regulations whenever I wanted to get out of the camp. Interpreters and translators were especially vulnerable. They were being hunted down and slaughtered like animals. It wasn't a fate I would choose, but I also wanted to spend some quality time with my grandmother without the soldiers sitting in the next room. I wanted to hear more of the family history that she'd been dripping into my consciousness like Tawoos dripped rose water into cold drinks. My grandmother told her stories, and I listened and memorized them. When she got tired of talking, she'd let out a sigh and look at me like someone waiting for a miracle. Did she expect me to suddenly get up and start shouting Down with America?

When the doctor told her that she needed an operation to replace a damaged knee joint, I quickly put a plan in place. Grandma would have her operation in Jordan, where there were probably more Iraqi surgeons than in Iraq anyway, hundreds of them who'd escaped death threats and settled in Amman and Dubai and Damascus and Sanaa. I'd get my two weeks leave from the army and we'd make our way separately and meet there. Two weeks would just be enough to spend some quality time with my grandmother. As it turned out, it was also enough for Muhaymen's name to become forever engraved on my soul.

I knew that he was the son of Tawoos, the woman who breastfed me when my mother fell ill with typhoid, and so he was another one of my milk brothers, but I hadn't understood "milk brother" thing. When Muhaymen appeared before me like a truly-aimed arrow, I was still wondering how Grandma could put her trust in a man from the Mahdi Army to bring her to Amman? Apparently Haydar's Arak-drinking habits had got him into trouble, now that Sadr City had become an ultra-conservative stronghold, and he'd gone into hiding for a while. So Muhaymen volunteered to step in for his brother and take the old Christian woman to Amman for treatment. They would cross the country road that passed through the Triangle of Death. He'd stay with Rahma until she got her treatment and saw her granddaughter who had come especially from America, and then he'd drive her back to Baghdad. It was this last-minute arrangement that shook the tree of my life and chased away the ravens of gloom that had nested in its branches.

Muhaymen stirred some deep currents in my soul. I wasn't young or naive enough to fall in love at first sight, but his name—he who rules over everything—was a beautiful omen and accidental trap. Besides, my stay in Amman, away from army restrictions and safe from the life-threatening dangers of Baghdad, put me in a pleasant state of giddiness. I was making a game out of hiding my army job from my neighbors and from Muhaymen, enjoying the pretence of being simply an Iraqi exile, homesick for her country and her people.

Muhaymen!

I fell in love with his name before I fell in love with him. His name was the hook, and with his intensity and his special way of talking he pulled me into the unique weave of his character. When I wrote about him, words came to me naturally, without need of the author's help! Did I love him for his qualities or was I simply testing my capacity to get close to my enemy? What film was it where the hostage fell in love with her abductor?

But I wasn't his hostage. I sleepwalked to his deep river and dove without fear into its silty waters. I was putting my trust in my enemy and falling in love with my brother. What would I write to Calvin now that this wave had overtaken me?

XXV

"Muhaymen, where did you get this strange name?" I asked him, before taking a puff from my nargila at Kan Zaman Café in Amman. My legs were stretched on a low wicker chair.

"What's so strange about it, dear sister? Muhyamen is one of the ninety-nine holy names of Allah. Our father chose for each of the eight of us a name with a religious meaning. It was my destiny to get Abdul-Muhaymen."

Muhaymen didn't smoke, but his very words were like flames rising from his chest. I wasn't used to hearing a man speak of destiny, the decreed, fortune, fate, what's written. It was something that belonged to my mother and my grandmother and Tawoos. His faith and his words were against me, standing between me and my fantasy, aborting my hopes. Did I need destiny to explain that I came to this part of the world, that I met Muhaymen and fell for him? I came here of my own volition, walking on these two legs that were as strong as the legs of mountain women.

"You could be one of Gaugin's models, you know," Calvin had said one day as we skimmed through a book about the

French painter in Detroit Public Library. I looked at the paintings with the bright colors spread on the pages before me and knew what he meant. The dark-skinned legs of the women in these paintings looked as if they were cast in a straight mould, without curves that start soft-fleshed at the thighs and end up narrow at the ankles. I felt a flash of gratitude for Calvin for putting an arty slant on something that I considered one of my faults, for creating a lineage for me that I hadn't been aware of.

So, with legs fit for a model from a tropical island, I walked to Muhaymen, waving the leaf of my seduction in his face, knowing full well it had thorny ends. I didn't hide my feelings but pursued them, expecting their blossoms of delight to start growing slowly from the pores of my skin. But Muhaymen didn't see my leaf or my blossoms. He just saw the thorns and shuddered, reacting as if we were partners in a crime of which I was ignorant.

"No way. It's impossible. You are my milk sister."

"What if I tell you that I don't believe in any of that milk nonsense?"

"So what, to me you're still my sister."

"Go fuck yourself then."

"Shnou?"

I was relieved he didn't understand, and instead of repeating the insult in Arabic, I bit my lip and went quiet. He was probably the first man in my life to make me feel shy. With others I'd felt bolder, cussing and swearing as much as they did or more. He possessed a kind of dignity that made me check myself. That nervous slender, bearded man who marched under the flag of a backward sectarian movement had managed to confuse me and exercise over me the power of love. One look from him was all it took for me to swallow my voice and rein in my loose tongue.

There was no doubt that it was my army job that armored me with my lexicon of obscenities. His brother Haydar had a point when he reluctantly confronted me with what my grandmother had said: that I was, God forbid, *tarbiya siz*. The reason, according to her, was that that faraway country had taken away my good manners and made me into someone else. Haydar said he disagreed, but promised out of courtesy to help her put me back on the righteous path.

Poor Haydar. The old woman wanted his help to return me to her Iraqi righteous path, not to my American one. To the righteousness of what was proper, of modesty, shyness, and tradition. She believed those values were hers alone, particular to her nation and excluding all others. A kind of blind Bedouin patriotism that would celebrate with gunshots if she saw me take my brother's side against my cousin, and my cousin's side against a stranger.

I was a stranger even to my grandmother, my mother's mother. Haydar and Muhaymen and Tawoos were closer to her than me because, like her, they'd remained pure Iraqis, like pure gold. Their patriotism wasn't tainted by a dual nationality, and the blood still raced in their veins when they heard the name Iraq, their unique glimmering planet in the midst of dark galaxies. They sang for Baghdad with the transcendence of whirling dervishes, their voices going hoarse with prayer, like they were reaching out to a remote paragon, their souls gazing towards it: the City of Peace, the Circled One, the Powerful One, Home of the Thousand and One Nights. *Baghdaaaaaad*, the Fortress of Lions.

I'd seen them at weddings in Detroit and Chicago and San Diego, the immigrants who still hung by an umbilical cord to their motherland, ready to sway their heads and shed a tear with the first tune of a patriotic song.

If you lose a homeland, where will you find another?

They seemed to secretly enjoy the heartache.

Oh birds in the sky, fly to my people.

Why had they come to America then? Why had they come with Iraq smuggled in their pockets like a drug that they couldn't quit? My mother would put the tape in the car stereo, her frown forming before the song even started.

Leaving was no stranger to you, no, no. It wasn't strange to see you go.

She'd cry and the tears would cloud her eyes, making me concerned we'd have an accident. I'd tell her it should be illegal to sell this tape without a health and safety warning. She'd look away and continue to sing along and cry.

Your mother's milk will lead you home.

But it wasn't my mother's milk that led me back to Baghdad. Tragedy had driven me away, and tragedy brought me back.

Who had the right to pass judgement on me?

My father was no wiser than my mother. He'd sit in his new car, the one he'd be paying instalments on for the rest of his life. As soon as he'd turned the key in the ignition he'd reach for the CD. "My country is dear to me even if it makes me suffer." And he'd sway his head in appreciation and yearning at that early hour of the morning. Why, then, did you leave the country that was dear to you and bring us here? How could it be dear to you, Father, when it made you suffer, broke your teeth, terrorized you and spied on you, and let its corrupt dogs cook up their reports against you?

They were all crazy about Iraq, like the myth of *Majnun*, who goes mad for the love of Layla. They said that Layla lay dying in Iraq, an inherited phrase that they all repeated like a charm. But Layla didn't die, and they weren't cured of their love. And here he was, one of her crazy admirers sitting just an inch away from my desire in our apartment in Deir Ghbar and calling me sister. He had all the qualities of Iraqis who had been singed by the flame of eternity, half-gods and half-children, enchanters of women with their deep melancholy and their folk poetry, keepers of the secrets of the night, carriers of heavy burdens and the keys to paradise. Did he take me for an insensitive American who didn't comprehend the obsessions of victims of the Arab condition, didn't appreciate the eternal force of their poetry?

Muhaymen recited the first half of a verse from a pre-Islamic poem, and I surprised him by completing it for him. He talked to me about the Iraqi folk poet Muzzafar Al-Nawwab, and discovered that I had memorized his poems better than he had. He was happy that I shared his love of poetry, and hid his annoyance when I surpassed him to horizons he hadn't reached. Every time he would ask, "Where did you learn all this?"

If he only knew how my father had taught me, what rhetorical elegance had graced my childhood!

I told him, resting my hand on his tense arm, about the enthusiasm of TV presenter Sabah Behnam for the Arabic language, about his passion for classical poetry, and his store of love poetry that had turned my mother's head until she could see no man but him. When she'd insisted on marrying him, my grandfather had told her, "But he's an Assyrian. What business does he have with us Arabs?"

"I don't care if he's Assyrian or Martian. I love him and I won't marry anyone else."

My mother, the daring one among the family's girls, made her choice and paid the price. My attraction to Muhaymen hadn't yet carried me to the heights that my mother reached when she fell in love with my father. I'd never loved a man to the extent of believing a pomegranate wasn't a pomegranate unless I ate it from his hand. But this slender Iraqi wasn't extending his palm to me with the red pearls of any fruit. He was stubbornly refusing to compromise beliefs that meant nothing to me. How could this Sumerian sculpture with the vague features be my brother just because Tawoos took me to her breast when I was two months old? He rejected my love but had no objection to my helping his brother Haydar escape to America by marrying him on paper. For him, I was no more than an American lifejacket to rescue his drunken brother from the pious militias to which he himself belonged.

Muhaymen's eyes widened in panic when I told him I didn't believe in milk that made siblings out of strangers, or in marriage on paper, or in the prohibitions that stood in the way of desire. He didn't understand that a free woman like me would only need him to bring the coal of his eyes closer for the sparks to turn into flames and the taboos to collapse.

I said to him, with a diabolical coquettishness that I wasn't used to in myself, "I want to find a husband here and live like a tame cat at his feet."

"You? A tame cat?"

"Even if it's only a temporary 'pleasure marriage.'"

"These things are not done, Zeina. Where did you learn such talk?"

"Isn't that what men here do? Don't other women accept it?"

The anger in his eyes made them darker and more beautiful. Looking at his face, I was lost in a sea of raw bronze. Did they flash like this, the eyes of Sumerian sculptures? His anger couldn't have been neutral or disinterested. My instinct told me that he wanted me even more than I wanted him. I swayed with my desire on the edge of the abyss, then tumbled down feeling light as a feather.

XXVI

We sat on the top floor of Al-Quds Restaurant, like any couple from a conservative family, and ordered kebab and yogurt. It was hot and the place was crowded with people running errands downtown. Judging by their accents, the majority were Iraqis either living in Amman or passing through it. The waiter showed us upstairs to the family section. I was being treated as his family, and my grandmother's operation had been successful and she would be leaving the hospital in a couple of days, so I was happy.

I didn't attempt to light a cigarette in case it disturbed him. I knew that men here didn't like women who smoked. And I was here in a man's company. He walked in front of me and chose the table, took the seat facing people, leaving me to look at the wall. It was he who talked to the waiter and ordered our food, asked where the restrooms were, then indicated to me with the corner of his eye that it was down the corridor on the right. I didn't complain. On the contrary, I, who'd always been the ringleader, planning trips and booking restaurants and deciding who sat next to whom, was enjoying the fact that someone else was taking over.

I ate like I'd just emerged from a famine. Muhaymen's company increased my appetite. He tore the flat bread with his hands, gave me one half and murmured "*Bismillah*."

"The kebab here is so tasty," I said.

"Not as tasty as the kebab in Karbala, or the pickles in Najaf."

"Leave your sectarianism out of it and just enjoy your food," I said gently, and he smiled obediently. Our whispered tones made me feel a certain intimacy between us, as if we were a couple on honeymoon who had come to Amman for a breath of fresh air. My unattainable fantasies were all I got from him, but they sufficed. I was a soldier facing death and hanging on to life by a thread.

We went out in the sun, headed to Amman's Third Circle neighborhood and entered a quiet coffee shop. Muhaymen took me from market to restaurant to coffee shop, just to avoid being alone with me in the apartment. When I got tired he sent me back by taxi and took his time following. When he did come to the apartment, he went straight from the front door to his room, walking quickly, almost running, and closed the door behind him. I stayed in front of the TV, a secret joy dancing in my chest, because if he really felt he was my brother he wouldn't have worried about being alone with me.

Once we were coming out from seeing my grandmother when he met a friend in the hospital corridor. Like all conservative men, he ignored my presence completely and took his friend aside without introducing him to me. They asked each other how they were doing, then I caught a few sentences in another language, which I recognized as Farsi, because one of my school friends was an Assyrian from Iran.

One afternoon he took me to a café on the Airport Road and let me order a mint-flavored nargila. Watching the clouds of smoke I exhaled, he started to whisper something that gradually got louder until I could make out the words:

My love is like wedding silver.
My love is like a nargila adorned
With turquoise water,
Alight with beauty.
Oh train, slow down, won't you?
Let my sad song call
To the desert bird in its flight.

I knew this poem by Muzaffar word for word, but coming from Muhaymen it sounded so much sweeter. I was easily charmed by beautiful words, and it made me happy that he was reciting poetry to me. If this wasn't flirting, what would be? But he didn't allow my happiness to last. Sometimes he would treat me like a tourist.

"You foreigners like to smoke the nargila because it's exotic."

"I'm not a foreigner."

"Your name is Zeina but you're American."

"And your name is Muhaymen but you speak Farsi."

His surprise didn't show, but I saw a muscle twitch in his left cheek before he let out a broken sigh and said, "I learned it when I was a prisoner of war in Iran."

How much time would I need to know him with all his history?

How many notebooks would he have to fill to know me with my past and my present?

I suddenly felt how ungenerous time was, and that what had passed of it shouldn't have passed. Not like this. The cafés of Amman were too narrow for our story. Their lazy rhythm couldn't carry the urgency that made our words race against their letters.

He was taken prisoner during the last year of the war with Iran. Fighting the war was not a choice he'd made. He'd been strolling with a friend on Saadoun Street when a military recruitment patrol simply lifted them off the sidewalk and threw them into the back of a truck that transported "volunteers" to the front lines.

"They just collected us from the street like municipal trucks collected garbage. I didn't volunteer, and I hadn't even finished my studies, but who listened to reason in those crazy times?"

The four years that Muhaymen spent in captivity turned him inside out. He went there a communist by birth and returned a religious man, who debated matters of heaven and hell.

I said to him, in an attempt at sympathy, "But your core must have stayed the same."

"The one thing that stayed the same was my hatred for Americans."

I let the hose of the nargila drop from my hand.

We spent our days walking around Amman and avoiding the apartment. We left early to go to the hospital to check on Grandma, then went to The Gardens Hotel for breakfast. Muhaymen drove us to Abdoun, and we left the car to walk around the quiet neighborhood. We pushed our hands deep into the pockets of our coats and watched the patches of snow that adorned the city's hills.

We talked about our past lives, each of us trying to gather a whole history into a small capsule for the other to swallow, so we could rest from talking. I was in a hurry, and my time was not my own. I knew that my days in Amman were numbered and that the Zone awaited me. My gilded cage that protected me from murderers and ambushes. I wondered if my killer would be Muhaymen or one of his comrades, a wild thought that placed me on the edge of a great abyss. A masked mujahid, like the ones I'd seen on extremist websites, walks towards me and, as soon as he's near me, stabs me in the side. I cling to him as I fall to the floor and uncover his face. I smile, content that death has visited me from his hand. He removes my helmet and lets out a silent scream when he realizes that the blood he's spilled is his sister's. It was a dream that I saw with my eyes wide open, my mouth dry and my hands stiffening, a Bollywood movie that was as yet untitled.

XXVII

L ayers of mist were peeling off our eyes like the layers of an onion. Tawoos would make sideways cuts in the onion with the knife, and then soak it in boiling water to make it easier to peel. It was the first step in the graceful waltz of cooking *dolma*. May I please have this dance?

The news and images that assailed us day in and day out were like hot water that peels off the layers of mist. But the waltz was no longer a gliding dance that twirls the soul to the tunes of violins made of ebony and rosewood. How long did it take us to understand that war was no dance and no picnic, that death had a bitter aftertaste?

The photograph of Regina Barnhurst in *USA Today* showed her sitting cross-legged on the green grass of Arlington Cemetery, as if she was on an idyllic "picnic" enjoying the fresh air and the spring sun. Her ginger locks fell on her face as she bent towards the inscription on a white headstone. The photographer seemed to have placed the camera at the lowest possible point before pressing the button. The picture had the same vantage point as the grass, growing with it in the shadow of the headstone.

Tommy brought us the newspapers tied with cotton twine. They stayed piled up in the corner, their smell reminding me of bagel shops on cold mornings. On each table a jar of honey and a newspaper. I cut the twine with the knife that I carried in my belt and checked the TV programs. What would my mother be watching tonight, over there?

It was Memorial Day, and the newspaper was flying its kite over the cemeteries and the grief-stricken homes. Nobody wanted to forget or help others forget. Photographers flocked to the mothers and set up their cameras on the doorstep of their tears. People liked to read about grief, and this woman was too weak to fight the readers' requests. Regina, or Gina, as they called her, came here every Sunday, spread a blanket on the grass and sat cross-legged, writing letters to Eric Herzberg, her son who was buried under the headstone, one of thousands of identical headstones that were lined up as far as the eyes could see in Section 60 of the cemetery. Underneath every one of them lay a soldier killed in Iraq.

Gina didn't lift her head to look at the women and men who wandered in silence among the graves. But Leesa Philippon saw her from a distance and felt an urge to get closer to her grief. She approached Gina and touched her shoulder. The visitors to cemeteries communicated by touching each other's shoulders. It was the sign of a common grief. They were like a group of blind people stepping into traffic, each one guided by the shoulder of the one before them.

Gina had lost her son, the marine lance corporal, to a sniper's bullet in the third year of the war. Leesa lost her son Lawrence in combat near the Syrian border on Mother's

Day of the same year. A hand guided by a shoulder that was crushed by suppressed grief. Weeping openly would not befit the mothers of national heroes.

Gina had nothing to say to the newspaper reporter who intruded on her quiet grief. Her tears were just drops in the sea of the cemetery. Maybe the other visitors would be more eloquent, she thought, but he insisted on hearing her. So she told him she empathized with the grief of Iraqi mothers that she saw on the news wearing black abayas and weeping over the children they lost in the streets of Baghdad.

That was another story. The reporter left Regina Barnhurst and went to Leesa Philippon. She and her husband drove seven hours to come to Arlington Cemetery. She'd wake up early on the designated day, get dressed and put on a little make-up, then sit in the car as if she was going to work.

Here, a stone's throw away from Congress and the White House, Leesa met dozens of grieving mothers and formed a club for the families of soldiers who'd died in Iraq. More mothers had joined since. Mother, may I please have this dance?

Beth Bell met Leesa Philippon in this club. Their sons were buried side by side. When Lawrence Philippon was killed, Captain Brian Letendre delivered the news to Leesa and her husband. They'd invited him to sit in their living room, and offered him coffee. But the captain didn't stay long. He had more news to deliver to other families. He'd come from Baghdad on a short break and hadn't seen his own two children yet. The Philippons became friends with Captain Letendre and his family. Soon it was his turn. He was killed in a suicide bombing in Iraq and was buried two rows away from Lawrence's grave. Officers came from Iraq every day carrying the news of death and brand-new boxes wrapped in the flag. The war went on, reaping its harvest. The club continued to grow, and new grieving mothers kept joining.

The grass grew greener in Arlington, the national cemetery. Four million tourists came here every year. They walked past the Tomb of the Unknown Soldier, smiled into small digital cameras and cellphones, and stood a while by President Kennedy's grave. They looked at his photo and thought of how Jackie stood here before them, how their footsteps might coincide with hers. "Great footsteps coincide," as my father used to say.

It was sometimes impossible to tell those visiting Section 60 apart from the tourists who filled the place. The mourners watched the cameras and sports caps, the water bottles peeking out of light backpacks, the pointed cellphones in every hand taking snapshots of the unending rows of white headstones. Domino pieces engraved with names and dates instead of black dots. The tourists went back to the buses that awaited them in the car park. The mourners remained sitting by the headstones, standing guard over the heads of the absent. Those absent from roll-calls in the camps in Iraq now lay in sixty-five cemeteries across America. Though silent, they were still a source of embarrassment. How many headstones were there in Detroit so far?

I didn't want to see my mother sitting on the grass like Gina, her white-streaked hair falling across her face, smoking and coughing by my grave. I would stop reading the newspapers from now on. They brought only sadness. War was nothing but a rotten onion.

XXVIII

Muhaymen lectured me with theories about how emigration created a rupture in the migrant's spirit. He kept asking me questions about my life in the US. There were five million Iraqis who'd left the lives they knew and fled into the unknown, and that concerned him. He thought emigration was like captivity: both left you suspended between two lives, with no comfort in moving on or turning back. I saw it differently. I told him that in this day and age, migration was a form of settling, that belonging didn't necessarily come from staying put in one's birthplace.

Muhaymen was astonished by people like me, who were able to settle as immigrants. He called us "skin changers." I didn't like his rigid judgements, so I protested, "I only have one skin. It just has multiple colors."

"Is your name Zeina or Chameleon? I only know the motherland, and I can't imagine having a stepmother land. I find the idea of a second homeland ridiculous."

"But the whole world can be your homeland. Haven't you

heard the expression 'citizen of the world?'"

He looked at me with resigned pity, as if he was watching a straw being tossed by the wind and looking for a tree to hang on to. He started to whisper words I couldn't at first make out. They were extracts from poems he had composed while in prison. Because he hadn't been allowed any paper, he'd memorized them. The poems were gentle in parts, and in others they were mysterious, more like prayers or riddles, talismans designed to mislead the prison guards. Do prisoners fear that their captors can read their minds?

I could only respond to Muhaymen with the poems memorized from my childhood. We were taking refuge in poetry, because direct flirtation was not allowed. So I retrieved verses that Dad used to recite as we sat for breakfast in the garden. My father liked Al-Jawahiry when he was drunk, and was inclined towards the Mahjar poets when sober. He liked the elegance of their language, which was fit for a presenter of literary programs. As we dipped our bread in our morning tea, my father, the renowned presenter, recited poetry and read in our eyes the impact of his voice. He trained his voice at our breakfast table, and we listened as we ate, or listened and forgot to eat, my mother's breath always trembling when he recited "Tigris of Goodness."

Were all those morning lessons in vain? Did my father teach me the language and train me in careful pronunciation so that I could end up an accredited interpreter for the US Army? I suppressed these thoughts, just as Muhaymen had hidden his thoughts from his captors. I feared that he could hear what was on my mind. He seemed happy with me and looked surprised when I recited a classical poem, waving my forefinger to punctuate the words as a sign of gravity. I was following the example of Sitt Gladys Youssef, my poetry teacher at school. He said I reminded him of the orators of Najaf, and although Najaf was a Shia city, and Gladys an obviously Christian name, he jokingly added, "Did Miss Gladys come from Najaf by any chance?"

We giggled together like two carefree lovers. So he *did* have a sense of humor! With just some basic training, he'd be completely my type. But he gathered the net quickly and re-gained his earnestness. I couldn't indulge my fantasies for long.

I was aware of my self-censorship as I told Muhaymen about myself and my life. I told him about my father's good looks, my mother's cough and my brother's intoxicants, about the dullness of our home in Detroit after Dad left us and moved to Arizona. I came up with entertaining anecdotes from the many jobs I'd had: as a secretary at a tourism agency, an interpreter at an immigration agency, a babysitter, a radio presenter at a Chaldean station in Detroit.

"In Chaldean?" he asked.

"And in Assyrian too."

I told him everything but kept my current job secret. I used stories like fishing nets. I threw them in his direction and pulled him towards me. He was both heavy and weightless, surrendering and resisting at the same time, a swordfish trying to swim against the net and being let down by the current. But the bronze face darkened when I got to the story about Calvin, my American boyfriend that my mother couldn't stand.

"Your mother must be right."

"Why do you say that when you don't even know him?"

"Do you love him?"

"I don't know. We've been together for four years."

"What do you mean 'together'?"

Oh, the sweet taste of jealousy!

Those were the first signs of a shift in my milk brother's feelings. All I had to do now was stir the coals to heighten the flames. Did I have to wear khaki, join an army and go to war in order to meet him? How much of my life had been wasted until then! Detroit. Green Cards. The rotting wooden houses of Seven Mile. Big paper cups of lukewarm coffee. Fancy cars bought on credit. Rental wedding suits and evening gowns. Virgin brides shipped over from the northern villages to the faraway continent. Grocery stores protected from theft by machine guns. The stores that immigrants dreamed of owning. The impoverished rich who gained money only after hard labor had cost them their health. They went home at the end of the night drained and barely able to recognize their families.

I left all that behind and came here to find him, only for a sip of breast milk to stand between us. But he was open for cheating. He rejected me for himself but offered me to his brother Haydar in a sham marriage that would let me take him along to the US, like a carry-on bag. What would I do with Haydar once we got there? What would he do with me? He would get his Green Card, plant a thank you kiss on his "dear sister's" forehead, then the vast continent would swallow him up.

"Muhaymen, why don't *you* come with me to America?"

"What would I do there, my dear sister? Work on a taxi between Dearborn and Detroit?"

This black sarcasm that clung to every Iraqi cut through me. It was as if they'd all lived through so much and couldn't see more life beyond the ruins of experience. As if Muhaymen could smell, from here, the disappointment that awaited him over there. He rejected my invitation and didn't want to see that, with me by his side, he wouldn't have to suffer like other immigrants had suffered.

Listen to me, my brother, my lord, my love, I can assure you that you won't be standing in line for the food stamps that are handed out to the disabled and the unemployed.

"What's wrong with food stamps, Sitt Zeina? Twenty million Iraqis lived on them for twenty years. They were called rations then."

It made me happy when he called me "Sitt Zeina." But conversation didn't flow easily between us. He would get into his sarcastic mode and start to deride everything I said. Then he'd notice I was upset and attempt to placate me by calling me "dear sister," which made my blood boil. With these two words, he turned himself into my legal chaperone and put up a veil between us that defined the space in which each of us moved. It was a statement or prohibition, like "No Smoking."

"Dear sister" was flat and vague, a metaphor that led to hell or a talisman that protected from sin. He used it for his own sake, not mine. By uttering those words, he became more resistant to my seduction, and at the same time extended a bridge from his blood to mine. When I heard them, the tide of my melancholy rose and carried me closer to insecurity. I hated the position he put me in and cursed the day that brought me back to this country.

XXIX

Death sat on the edge of our beds; it planted itself under our pillows and settled at our feet.

It spared me, not taking me seriously enough, but it took its time selecting our best soldiers.

Death had extravagant taste.

I passed by the medical clinic on my way to work and saw the guards pull a stretcher out of a truck with a corpse covered by a sheet or an army jacket. There were always other soldiers standing on the side, smoking gloomily and rubbing their eyes. I didn't know who the victim was this time and was afraid to ask. A gray mist covered my eyes. My tears flowed inwards.

Death was coming closer. It started attaching its black ribbons to names I knew. People with whom I had shared meals. Charlie was killed by a roadside bomb. He was a civilian, an ex-marine, contracted by the army to drive local translators from one camp to the other. I didn't know about his death until days later. At first I thought he was away on a mission, until his sister went on his email and sent a note to all his contacts. She told us that his body had been blown apart a few miles south of Mosul.

The situation in Mosul wasn't any different from other cities. People woke up in the morning to find severed heads thrown in public squares. It was a terror familiar to the city's memory. The difference was half a century. Old people remembered the end of the '50s and shook their heads. Cities were cutting their own heads off at the hands of their children.

I found utter chaos when I reached Mosul. Police stations were bombed and closed down. Masked men were roaming the streets. Was this the city of my ancestors that made my heart flutter at the mention of its name?

A new Iraqi military unit, called the Wolf Brigade, was created to bring the situation under control. It was one of the units we formed to work with our troops. They chased insurgents from street to street in the hope of returning order to the city. We called them insurgents, rebels, terrorists, criminals, or troublemakers, anything to avoid using the word "resistance."

I was in Mosul for my second Christmas in Iraq. Four days earlier, a suicide bomber had entered Ghazlany, the camp where I was staying near Mosul Airport, and had blown himself up in the food hall, in the midst of soldiers eating their lunch. Twenty-two people died, among them fourteen from our forces and four Iraqi soldiers. Fifty-one Americans were injured. The suicide bomber had been vetted by our security, which meant we trusted him and counted him as one of us. He had smuggled the explosives into the camp incrementally. That same evening, one of the local religious groups claimed responsibility for the bombing and applauded it as an act of resistance. Just a different point of view, according to political analysts and the research centers' brainboxes. What was happening in Iraq had happened in France and in Vietnam, predictably exaggerated according to the more radical temperament in the region. Weren't we told that no war resembled another?

I didn't hear the sound of the explosion in my room, but heard the missiles that followed, launched from outside in the direction of our rooms. Our bedrooms were metal wagons called "hawks," twenty feet by eight. We slept in cages like monkeys.

One of the missiles landed on the room across from mine. The shock of the explosion threw me down on my back. The sergeant who lived in the room had gone to brush his teeth. He narrowly escaped death in the cage.

There was a church set up in Ghazlany for Sunday mass. On the Sunday following the bombing, the church was full. The priest was wearing a white embroidered cloak, his khaki pants showing underneath. My inner jinni came and sat beside me, looked at the priest's legs and asked, "Where do you think he's put his helmet?"

"Under the altar."

"Wrong. Can't you see it hanging on the cross?"

There was an African-American soldier playing the guitar together with a Gospel choir. I pushed my jinni away and closed my eyes, abandoning myself to the voices that carried good tidings and soothed my loneliness and grief. I'd spent the previous night writing an article and emailing it to all my friends. I told them about the history of Mosul, its geography, about the twisted minaret. I explained a little bit about my job, in general terms. I'd write a sentence then delete it to steer away from security prohibitions. I wrote that my work was exciting but could be depressing. I didn't write that it depressed me to interpret the vague sentences that were part of a language mastered by those detained for acts considered rebellious, the majority being poor and desperate young men. They refused to cooperate and answered questions with an invariable "Wallah I don't know." The American soldiers had learned these words having heard them so many times, and started to use them among themselves. Tommy or Michael or Deborah would spread their palms, turn down their lower lips, shake their head and say in laughable Arabic, "Wallah I don't know. Don't know anything."

One time, when the officer went out and left me alone with an elderly detainee, he faked a gentlemanly smile and asked me, "Where is Sister from?"

"I'm American."

"But your accent is from Baghdad."

"Yeah, I was born in Baghdad."

"And why do you work with the occupiers of Baghdad?"

I cut the conversation short. "You're not allowed to speak when the officer is not present."

Before I was sent to Iraq, the woman officer who conducted my security interview had asked me, "If the terrorists kidnap you and threaten to torture you, what secret information would you be willing to give them?"

"I'd shove my shoe up their asses," I had replied with utter seriousness. She wasn't shocked at all and seemed to like my answer.

But my army years passed and I didn't have to face a situation like that. The only time I felt threatened was when I passed a cell occupied by a dangerous detainee on my way to the bathroom. He looked out through the bars of the tiny window gesturing with his thumb across his neck, threatening me with slaughter. I didn't respond, but continued on my way, peed, washed, and then called two particularly tough soldiers and asked them to teach him a lesson. I didn't bat an eyelid.

The brutality of our soldiers increased in direct proportion to our losses. The sight of stretchers carried in and out of the clinic became a daily routine, but I still couldn't get used to it. It was in this atmosphere of fear, with death lurking around every corner, that the case of Abu Ghraib dropped on us.

I was busy interpreting at the airport prison when I saw the pictures on TV. Fox News was on, and I saw the footage without sound. I abandoned what I was doing, walked to the TV, and turned up the volume. It felt a lot like the day I had seen the attack on New York. I experienced a few moments of paralyzed shock. I looked around and saw a few soldiers and officers, all nailed to the spot and watching. The news report came to an end. We looked at each other, as if we were seeking reassurance that we were far away from that prison and had nothing to do with what was happening there. I was searching my brain for the right term. Military honor. I used to be moved to tears when I read about it in novels or saw it in movies in a scene of a victorious military leader saluting his defeated enemy, or a soldier sacrificing himself for the flag, doing all he could to prevent it from touching the ground.

Abu Ghraib was a far remove from *The Bridge on the River Kwai*, and military honor was no longer just a male issue. There were women offenders too, and that made my anger more bitter. How did that bitch, who was dragging a prisoner behind her like a dog on a leash, get into our army?

Prisons were not suitable places for cinema, despite all the movies that were set in them. The real protagonist wasn't pain; it was humiliation. I thought about my father at Saadoun Security Complex, and imagined Private Lynndie England tying him by his neck with a dog leash and dragging him naked behind her. The gorge rose in my throat and my nose. How would I be able to face my dad?

The soldiers were talking about the images that kept being shown on TV. Some were resentful, and others were trying to find justifications. They said that such things were done by ignorant low-ranking soldiers. Someone called them "stupid" for allowing photos to be taken. Another answered in a deep voice that those prisoners must've been violent criminals to be treated that way.

I listened but felt unable to take part in the debate, until Shikho, one of our local translators, said something that struck me like a poisoned arrow.

"Guys, this is nothing compared to what used to happen in the Baathist prisons."

"Shikho, just shut your mouth," I found myself saying.

"Why are you so angry, Sitt Zeina?"

"Because our job here is not to replace torture with torture."

I addressed him in Arabic first, then I stood up and re-peated what I'd said in English in a voice loud enough for others to hear. They turned and looked at me like I was the spokesperson for the enemy—or for Amnesty International at best. I retreated into the metal cage that was my bedroom and stayed there until the following morning, a prisoner of my fury.

XXX

Christmas 2005 came and went while I was away from my grandmother. The big holidays were the markers by which I divided my years. My mood remained gloomy, in spite of the strings of shiny paper and glo-stars that decorated our green prison. Every evening I updated the hurried diary I was keeping on my laptop and wrote long emails to Calvin and my mother in Detroit. Occasionally I sent kisses to Dad in Arizona, to which he replied that e-kisses did not count. He worried because of the rising casualties among our soldiers in Iraq and wrote to me, "Come back on your own two legs before you are returned in a box. I wouldn't be able to bear it."

I wrote to Jason asking how he was doing in college, where he'd started a course in mechanical engineering, and he replied, "I thought about taking over your room to set up a ping-pong table. But I want you to come back. Do you think I'd be happy if I finished college and became an engineer, with your money, while you were lying under a marble cross, or dancing at your wedding with a wooden leg?" Even Jason, my stoner little brother, feared for my life. My absence had mellowed him, and he became sensitive like my mother. My mother's letters drowned me in misery. She seemed to be conspiring with my grandmother and Muhaymen against me. She wrote long essay-like letters that were like history lessons from the national education curriculum. But which of the two nations?

Sitt Batoul sent her letters by post, because she still didn't take email seriously. She wrote on the paper of the hotel where she used to work. At the start of our life in America, she used to customize pants for Walmart, shortening the legs according to customers' demands, for two dollars a pair. It was a job she was forced to take on when my father suffered a heart attack, five months after we arrived in the country. The former TV presenter couldn't bear carrying beer boxes at a storehouse owned by relatives—millionaires who hadn't finished school.

At the hotel, Mom worked in the kitchen for three years, and was then transferred to reception. She cursed her bad luck every day, until she ran into the former Head of the Philosophy Department at the University of Baghdad arranging vegetables at Farmer Jack's. Dr. Yaqoub explained to her, not without some pride, how he preserved lettuce heads by trimming the outer leaves and dipping the tips in cold water. His efforts earned him the praise of his supervisor and a raise of fifty cents per hour. After that encounter, Sitt Batoul stopped complaining and was content with her job. But then she lost it when the hotel was turned into a "smoke-free zone," her cigarette being a sixth finger on her right hand.

So she wrote to me on the old hotel paper asking me to go and visit the convent school. It was in a yellow stone building at the Eastern Gate, built on a piece of land that the king of Iraq had presented to a French mission in the twenties. That's how

145

she described it in the letter. But I didn't need directions to find the school where we, both my mother and I, had studied. She told me about the nuns at the school and about the girls they taught who went on to serve the country. I thought I could detect the fingerprints of Grandma Rahma between the lines. Had my mother too been recruited to the project of my re-education?

There was a greeting card accompanying the letter, with a picture of a snow-covered field. The snow was glittering specks decorating the card, like sugar that tempted you to lick it. It was nothing like that white messy substance that gathered outside the front doors in Detroit, which we had to shovel away every morning before starting the car. The cards I got from my parents didn't lessen my loneliness at Christmas, nor did the emails from Calvin and the rest of the gang. I went out in my armored vehicle and saw the Christmas trees being sold on the sidewalks of Elweyya and Palestine Street. The cedars were carried away in cars' half-opened trunks to homes I knew nothing about.

The cars slowed down when the drivers glimpsed us approaching in their rearview mirrors. They pulled in off the road, onto the sidewalk, to let us pass, and waited with anxious eyes. They said nothing, their hearts remaining closed. Could they enjoy the festivities, those eyes that went to sleep on terror and awoke to terror?

I told myself it wasn't me they feared but my uniform. It wasn't by chance that I felt something like masculinity the first time I put on the army uniform. It added dimensions to my character that disappeared when I took it off. I stood taller, held my shoulders back, and felt my chest grow broader. I put on the helmet with the patterned net and the mirror sunglasses and turned from a slightly-built, dark-skinned woman into an alien from outer space. The aliens moved around in groups, rode in Hummers, and carried the latest guns. Everything in the street made way—pedestrians and ambulances and horse-drawn carriages. People watering their gardens shrunk back into their houses.

The scene froze while our convoy drove past, like someone had pressed the pause button. Boys squeezed the brakes on their bicycles and stopped with one foot on the ground. Cars stuck to the dusty edge of the road. Pedestrians stood still. It was as if everyone was observing a minute's silence. Who were they mourning?

At first I used to smile at people on the street. Some children smiled back, but the adult faces revealed something else. Then facial expressions changed. They wore something like a look of disgust. Did we smell? The garbage was piling up on every corner, and with time, disgust turned into hatred. Someone had distributed theater masks with evil faces to everyone in the city.

"They hate us," my companions in the car said from behind the helmet straps that covered their mouths, but I refused to believe it. I convinced myself that I was exempt. I was born in Iraq, and I had the same skin color, the same language, and the same fiery temperament as these people. They couldn't hate me. "Can't you see that they hate you even more than they hate us?" Deborah was telling me only half the truth. The whole truth was that Iraqis thought of my comrades as the foot-soldiers of the occupation, merely performing their military service and following orders. They had no say in the war. In a way, they were like Iraqi soldiers in the Iran–Iraq War and the Kuwait invasion. But they saw me as a traitor.

My eyes were suddenly opened to a depressing picture. Was that how my grandmother saw me? And Tawoos? And Haydar?

What about Muhaymen? Would he hate me and wish me dead? I had a dream about him the other night. He kidnapped me and took me to an unknown place, not into the forest on a white horse like a knight who had eloped with his beloved, but to his group in the Mahdi Army with my hands tied and my mouth gagged in the trunk of a white Toyota. I was blindfolded, so I couldn't see him, but I recognized his smell in their midst. Even scents came to me in my dreams. I woke up thirsty and suffocating with grief.

I didn't mind when my contract with the army came to an end soon after Christmas. It was time for me to go back to Detroit. But I saw it as just a break. I didn't think my life there would go back to normal. My life was broken in two: "before Baghdad" and "after Baghdad." I was confused and felt that this wasn't yet the end of the story.

I wasn't sad, but I didn't have a happy Christmas. We were inventive with our parties and gave each other unusual presents. I gave Captain Donovan an old Elvis disk that had belonged to my Uncle Munir and which I had found at my grandmother's house. He gave me a colored dish plaited out of palm leaves, with a blue eye design at the center. Deborah gave me a scarf made of soft black cotton, like the ones Iraqi women used to cover their heads, that she had embroidered herself with red and yellow flowers. But all that did nothing to improve my mood.

On Christmas morning I got an email from Sad Malek saying that Condi was coming to visit Ghazlany camp, that she might share the traditional turkey meal with the soldiers. In the evening, he wrote again saying that the Secretary of State had come but had had lunch with the leaders of the Kurdish zone and just quickly passed by the soldiers. Then Rumsfeld arrived on another "surprise" visit. It was one Santa after the other. We knew about his presence from TV and were told that he was meeting with the officers upstairs, in a part of the camp where interpreters weren't allowed. A Lebanese colleague left his position and managed to sneak upstairs and get his photo taken with the Secretary of Defense. In the days that followed he kept showing off the photo.

"If you'd come with me upstairs, you'd have had your own photo," he told me.

"You can shove it!"

XXXI

"A dog with two homes" was how Tawoos described me when I returned from Detroit to Baghdad. I couldn't get my old life back, and I couldn't adapt to my life in the Zone. I was a dog with two homes but unable to feel at home in either. Tawoos might've been unpredictable and a bit crazy, but she sometimes spoke pearls of wisdom, especially when it came to diagnosing me. Her milk that ran in my veins guided her to the source of my problem. My grandmother said that I came to the world into the Tawoos's hands. She was the one who received me from Batoul's womb, tied the umbilical cord and washed away the blood. My mother used to say that Tawoos was a good person, but that she was ignorant. She couldn't read or write and used her fingerprints to sign documents. So she never fully trusted her with me.

Tawoos had gone and enrolled for adult literacy classes, where she had to pay five dinars if she missed a day. Following the teacher's advice, she started to buy newspapers and was always seen with the *Jumhuriyya* under her arm. She sat in the front yard with her textbook and read out loud, "Rashid and Zeinab planted a tree." She studied for months, but then got bored and stopped, and the letters she'd learned flew out of her head. She kept buying the newspaper anyway, saying it was still useful for non-readers. It could be used to protect the head from the sun, placed at the edge of the sidewalk to sit on while waiting for the bus, and spread on the table at mealtimes. Who could object to Tawoos's wisdom?

I returned to Baghdad after a few months of feeling completely lost in Detroit. Tawoos came to visit me in the Green Zone and didn't like the state I was in. "A dog with two homes." I had called and asked her about Muhaymen. His cellphone was switched off and he didn't reply to my emails. She probably didn't know what email was. She told me that he'd gone to Najaf and that she was worried about him. Things were dangerous, and his group was wanted.

"Why did he go?" I asked.

"He went with his comrades. The world is on fire over there. May Allah protect them."

I had brought her presents from my mother, so I asked her to come and meet me. I was still jet-lagged when I greeted her at the gate. She had something of Muhaymen's scent. How could I see him? Did I dare invite him to the Zone?

My stay in Detroit hadn't been a vacation. I was impatient to get back to Iraq and searched frantically for another translation agency contract. I had to undergo the security checks and fill out the various forms all over again. I flew to Virginia and finished all the paperwork and met a new batch of translators. They were beginners and I was now the veteran.

I couldn't adapt to life without danger, couldn't adapt to my relationship with Calvin, and I couldn't stand by the window and contemplate the snowflakes falling outside. Contemplation wasn't for soldiers.

The plane that had taken me to my "home sweet home" was delayed in Frankfurt. We were told there was a snowstorm in Detroit. I shivered and was already overcome by a yearning for the Baghdad sun. We waited for a few hours before we could fly. I passed out in my plane seat, the exhaustion of all the past months suddenly catching up with me. It was a comfortable civilian plane, nothing like the hideous whale that had carried us in its belly to Iraq. I only woke up when the flight attendant tapped me on my hand. I looked for Calvin at Arrivals but couldn't see him. I borrowed a cellphone from a fellow passenger and called him, told him I was here, in Detroit. He answered as if I had just popped out to the store. What was wrong with him? I was returning from Hell. He knew what time I was arriving. Why was he yawning at the other end of the phone? Why couldn't he find anything more than "hi" to say?

"I thought you'd be at the airport."

"My car is out of gas, and there's snow blocking the roads."

I felt cold and lonely. I felt the same desolation that must eat into a soldier returning on crutches and dragging a damaged leg. There was nothing damaged in my body: the pain was in parts of my memory, and my green cloth bag was too heavy. People around me were running to their relatives and loved ones and hugging. Christmas decorations still dangled from the airport ceiling. I heard a familiar voice say my name.

I hadn't expected Jason to come and meet me, nor had I expected to see my father in Detroit. They walked over and showered me with hugs and kisses. I broke into tears, forgetting all about military toughness. I wasn't crying out of longing but out of gratitude. They rescued me from my loneliness, from the pain of the unresolved love I had left behind.

That evening my father opened a bottle of sparkling Italian wine as we gathered around the dinner table with my mother. She kept touching me to make sure I was really there and in one piece. She piled food onto my plate and sat there smoking and watching me. She ate nothing herself and avoided looking at Dad. We were gathered at home like we used to before their separation. This was the Christmas I had missed in Baghdad.

Dad had come for me and for news from the country he loved. He longed to hear it straight from my mouth, as if I knew more than what was in the media. He asked me about his old friends. Did any of them still read the news on TV? My father didn't realize that an earthquake had shaken everything over there. He spoke of Iraq as if it had been preserved in aspic since he left it. How could someone feel this longing for a country that had cruelly broken his teeth?

I told him about government buildings that had turned to ash and black ruins. How poverty-stricken women who had been widowed in earlier wars had taken their children and gone to squat in the empty buildings of the Ministry of Defense. About Iraqi military camps that had been deserted. The palaces of the government becoming the headquarters for opposition parties. And security forces collapsing, their informers escaping back to their villages. I told him how our army took charge of whole cities and started building everything from zero. On ground zero.

My father drank in silent sadness, finished the bottle and had two glasses of whisky. He listened to me until my mouth went dry and my voice went hoarse and he had grown tired of drinking. Then he stood up and, waving his finger in the Najaf style of recital, announced in his broadcasting voice, "Beware, beware the people of Iraq." Then he fell back on the sofa and passed out.

The following morning he said goodbye to us and headed back to Arizona. Jason drove him to the airport. I stayed with my mother, her eyes pursuing me, trying to get to the heart of the matter. She didn't buy what I had told them the previous night.

"Listen, Zeina. Everything you said yesterday, we already know all that from TV. Get to the point."

"Ok, Grandma is very upset. She didn't accept my going back this way."

"Your grandmother doesn't accept anything."

"She thinks you failed in bringing me up."

"That's how she is. Nothing ever pleases her."

"Can you believe that she concocted a plan with Tawoos and her son Haydar to brainwash me?"

"Tawoos? May Allah reward her and her children! If it wasn't for them, your grandmother would've died of loneliness."

"Did she really breastfeed me when I was little?"

"Oh yes, for two months, when I had typhoid and couldn't feed you myself. Her sons became your milk brothers."

My mother had gone straight to the point. Without realizing it and with the simplicity of stating my personal data. Birthplace: Baghdad. Hair color: black. Special characteristics: one brother in Detroit, six brothers in Sadr City.

XXXII

The exposed stone staircase hadn't changed. I climbed it lightly, as if my legs still belonged to that twelve-year-old girl. The wind blew in my face, and Sister Marie-Noelle walked in front of me without saying a word, as if she had taken a vow of silence. The rattling of her long prayer beads and her key chain, both hanging from her belt, lent their rhythm to our footsteps. How many schoolgirls had walked up these stairs before an exam, to pray at the small dark chapel on the school's rooftop? How sweet life was when exams were its main predicament. Things had got a bit more complicated since.

I stopped by the high concrete platform outside the chapel door. The railing around the rooftop came up to my waist. I gulped the fresh air as my eyes lingered on the view before me, canceling out the past twenty years since I had last stood there. I looked at the school buildings, with the windows of the nuns' rooms to the right and beyond them the city. The sun was beautiful, but the ruins in the center of Baghdad were depressing. I recognized the film: *King Kong in the City*.

On this terrace we used to crowd for a view of the real world outside, that world from which our parents struggled to protect us. They wanted to keep their daughters beyond the reach of experience and anguish. When our supervisors weren't looking, we would slow down at this spot, to look out over the whole area surrounding the Taqdomah Convent School at the Eastern Gate, which became known as Al-Aqida High School after nationalization. The pulsating traffic of Tahrir Square, the symbolic Liberty Statue, the grandness of the Ministry of Planning, and, over there, the magic of the Tigris with its rich mud color, the wooden boats and fishing nets, and all those men who walked hurriedly or strolled slowly by, only a reckless shout away. When one of us called out, the men would incline their heads towards the girlish voice, delicious anticipation in their eyes. I didn't like the phrase "those were the days," but that was what went through my mind as I stood on that spot.

Everything had changed in Baghdad except the churches. The smell of incense was the same, as if the stick I had lit myself fifteen years ago was still burning, or even the one lit by my mother twenty years earlier still. The nun confused me with my mother and called me Batoul. Wait here, Batoul. Kneel here, Batoul. Mind the step, Batoul. What difference would it make if I explained that Batoul was my mother and that I was her daughter Zeina? Ma Soeur Marie-Noelle lived largely in her own head, and my name did not feature there because I had been taught by another nun, whose name was Melena and who later left the convent for a man's love. She was visiting her village in the north of Iraq when she discovered that the new baker was more attractive than Jesus. She married him and left her long black habit to another woman who had never smelled the sweat of a man.

Accompanied by dread, I knelt before the Virgin's statue. She hadn't aged, nor had her white marble dress frayed. Its folds were still wavy, and the sky-blue belt still fluttered in the playfulness of an invisible wind. I marvelled at myself reciting the prayers in Arabic without mistakes or forgetfulness. I thought that praying was like cycling or swimming. We could abandon it for years but found the motions came back as soon as we entered the water.

Ma Soeur Marie-Noelle watched me with a suppressed smile. She whispered, so as not to disturb the silence of the saints hovering in the place, "Do you remember *The Praying Hands*, Batoul?"

"The what hands?"

"*The Praying Hands*, the book of prayers and supplications."

How could I forget? It was my story, not Batoul's, or was Ma Soeur playing on our memories? The Mother Superior had pulled me by my sleeve to her room one day and handed me a copy of *The Praying Hands*, telling me it was a new book she'd just received from Beirut. She said, "I was told you were good at Arabic and at recitation. I want you to read a prayer from this book every day at the morning prayer."

The book crowned me the princess of morning mass. The schoolgirls and the saints' icons stood in reverence, the sound of the rain and the ambulance sirens went quiet, the flames of the candles froze, while I delivered my recitation. "My Lord and my love. I longed for You and, in my loneliness, I prayed and beseeched You to have mercy upon me. You have not let me down, You whose mercy is vast, but took my hand through the dark maze, and it was suddenly flooded by Your light."

As I advanced through the school years, my power over the other girls grew. The power of religion had a special dynamic that I had not understood at that tender age. Today I'd readily take apart the authority of bishops, rabbis and ayatollahs, all those who hold people by the weakest points in their spirits: fear of fate and fear of death. Faced with those, the scared children of Adam are incapable of anything but blind obedience, the kissing of hands to escape expulsion from paradise.

For a while I enjoyed my growing spiritual status in the school. Other girls wanted me to touch their foreheads with my blessed hand before each exam. One of them asked permission to bring a small cassette recorder into church in order to record my readings and memorize them, and the tapes started circulating in the bags of the girls from our school and reached the convent schools of Wardiyya, Saint Joseph and the Morning Star. As I approached the end of the book, my throne was threatened. So I didn't tell the Mother Superior when I had gone through all the prayers in the book. Instead I started to compose my own prayers each evening, making sure they were similar in style to those of *The Praying Hands*. It wasn't easy to give up power. I understood that now.

We had come here like a giant bulldozer to topple the throne of a single man. I understood the meaning of power, even when it came to Grandma Rahma giving orders to her saints, raising their status when her prayers were answered and blacklisting them when she got no response. After we had all left the country and flown away from under her wing, her saints were all that remained under her power. She told me once she was looking in her prayer booklets for the name of the patron saint of migrants and couldn't find it.

"Do you want to ask him to take care of us?" I asked.

"No, I want to denounce you to him and implore him to remove his protective cloak and leave you all to stand exposed under foreign skies, for only then might reason return to your heads and return you to me."

That evening, after my visit to my school, I googled *Praying Hands*. Did it really exist or was it all a childhood illusion? I found the answer on the website of the Arabic Christian Encyclopaedia: The book was written by Michel Quoist, Arabized by Father Hector Al-Douehy, published by Al-Mashriq Press, Lebanon.

My father had picked it up once from my pillow, leafed through its pages and smiled an indecipherable smile. I had looked at him expectantly, waiting for a comment about the beauty of the prayers, but instead he had pointed out a grammatical error on the cover. Well, to each his own!

XXXIII

Two bullets in the head and four in the still hairless chest, which meant one bullet for every three years in the life of the young soldier. Deborah tied a yellow ribbon around the palm tree by the porch that we sat on to smoke. Most of the plants in the garden had died, but palm trees were made to live. Chris, our cook who knew nothing about cooking except how to fry chicken breasts, came over and sat on the dry grass hugging his guitar. He played the tune first then started to sing in a deep voice: *Tie a yellow ribbon round the ole oak tree.*

For two weeks we'd been waiting for news about three comrades kidnapped west of Mahmoudiyya. They'd been ambushed; four soldiers and an Iraqi interpreter had been killed in the attack and the rest had disappeared. Of those who were killed I only knew Younis the interpreter, a former English teacher at Farahidy School. Younis, Majnun Salma. He idolized Salma Hayek and carried a topless photo of her in his wallet, although he'd never seen any of her movies, since satellite channels were banned in Iraq and cinemas showed nothing but Indian movies.

Whenever Younis opened his wallet on cigarette breaks, we all knew that he was devouring Salma with his eyes.

"Where's Younis?" someone would shout, and another would answer, "He's stuck in Sadr City," *sadr* being the Arabic word for "breast." The soldiers' laughter would rise, and he would answer with literal translations of insults from colloquial Arabic. Comic swear words that we wouldn't hear again after Younis' death. Just as we would no longer hear him begging for a movie starring his idol, ordered by army post, because "the corrupt postmen would steal ordinary post."

The army promised a two-hundred-thousand-dollar reward for information about the missing soldiers. One of them was a young soldier from Michigan called Brian, not yet twenty. A sense of frustration reigned in the camp. Four thousand US Army personnel, along with two thousand from the Iraqi police force, went out to search for the missing soldiers in the Triangle of Death. The neighborhood of Basateen and Nakheel was located between Yusufiyya, Mahmoudiyya and Lutayfiyya, only half an hour south of Baghdad.

A few days later the Iraqi police found the body of a man in US Army uniform and with a tattoo on his right arm. The body was bloated, having been floating for at least two days among the weeds of the Euphrates. Lieutenant-Colonel Jocelyn Apperley, spokesperson for the Baghdad command, released a statement saying that the body belonged to Joseph Anzack Jr., one of the three missing soldiers. It had two bullets in the head and four in the chest. General Petraeus told the *Army Times* that he knew who was responsible for the kidnapping. It was an associate of Al-Qaeda.

Chris's singing was better than his cooking. The words he sang were those of a released prisoner to his sweetheart: He's heading home after three years in prison and doesn't know if she'll be waiting, so he asks her for a sign. If she still wants him, she'll tie a yellow ribbon to the old oak tree.

Deborah tied a yellow ribbon around the palm tree after she read that the schoolmates of the two soldiers who were still missing tied yellow ribbons around the trees on the two roads leading to their schools. The ribbons caught the imagination of the residents of Waterford, Michigan and Lawrence, Massachusetts. I didn't understand at first.

"Haven't you heard the song before?" Deborah asked.

"It sounds familiar. I think I've heard the tune before."

"Look it up."

When it was time for my nightly emailing ritual, I looked for the song and listened to the original version. It was sad in a hopeful kind of way. *Tie a Yellow Ribbon* was a folk song written by Irwin Levine and L. Russell Brown and sung by Tony Orlando and Dawn. It first came out in April 1973—that is before I was born. It topped the UK and US charts for four weeks and sold three million records. And it wasn't just a bubble either. The song returned to the radio eight years later, during the American hostage crisis in Tehran. The listeners liked it because it revived a nineteenth century tradition, when the lovers of American cavalrymen tied their braids with yellow ribbons as a symbol that they were waiting for someone's return. Yellow was the color of the cavalry. There was also a John Wayne movie inspired by that tradition. The yellow ribbon became the symbol for absent loved ones, whether in prison or in the Vietnam War. Now, in this war, it was a way to send a message that they would find arms open wide to receive them when they came home.

I clicked again, and what did I find? The song hadn't passed without controversy. In the fall of 1971, Pete Hamill, a commentator in the *New York Post*, wrote an article with the title "Going Home," in which he recounted the story of a high school student who sat next to a former prisoner on a bus. The boy was going on a school trip to the beach at Fort Lauderdale: the prisoner had just been released and was on his way home. Throughout the trip, he was anxious about finding a yellow handkerchief tied to the bark of an ancient oak tree. Hamill claimed to have heard this story through oral tradition. *Readers Digest* reprinted the article nine months later, in the summer of 1972. In the meantime, ABC adapted the story for the screen and gave the role of the returning prisoner to the actor James Earl Jones. All this happened before Levine and Brown copyrighted their song. When the song was released and became a huge success, Hamill sued them, claiming that he owned the copyright for the idea behind the lyrics. He wanted a share in the millions that the two songwriters made when they sang the tale of an ex-convict anxiously watching for a yellow ribbon around an old oak tree.

A third click brought up an amusing factoid: "During its popular years, tens of radio stations played this song regularly, until the number of times it was played reached three million. That is the equivalent of seventeen years of continuous airtime." But the fourth click was more important: a viral video of a satirical cover of the song by a band called Asylum Street Spankers. They changed its chorus line to "Stick magnetic ribbons on your SUV." That was their way of mocking the yellow ribbon magnets that had become fashionable to stick on cars, in support of the American soldiers fighting in Iraq. I looked for the ribbon on YouTube and listened to the Spankers, swaying with their rhythm and giving free reign to my melancholic mood. I could see a long chain of our soldiers' bodies lining the road from Hanoi to Baghdad. My Iraqi experience was starting to taste like vinegar.

XXXIV

I missed him and I had to see him. Hearing his news from Tawoos was no longer enough, and his emails didn't quell my longing. I wrote to him from the Green Zone and pretended that I was in Detroit. He said that he was writing from an internet café on Palestine Street, but I imagined that he was in one of the Mahdi Army hideouts. Our emails exhausted me more than they soothed me. He didn't believe I was in Detroit, and I didn't know where he was writing from.

When did Muhaymen detect the Green taint and find out that I was on the other side of hell? Or had he always known and played along, like an actor with a minor role? For his part, he had nothing to hide from me. Militias nowadays were replacing political parties in Iraq. Religious faith was the new politics, and everyone was sheltering under the umbrella of one group or another.

I think he was way cleverer than me. He understood once and for all that human beings are changeable and learned to embrace his own inconsistencies. Which of us was the chameleon? My supposed brother found the ultra-adjustment pill, swallowed it with a glass of water and went with the flow. Why should he be ashamed of the fact that he was a communist who turned Islamist? Or that he was a prisoner of war in Iran? Or that his younger brother worked with the intelligence of the former regime?

"Believe me, nobody's clean in Iraq today. The only difference is how much dirt each of us has swallowed."

"Wrong. There's still the faction of Grandma Rahma and her ilk."

I went to the top of the screen and clicked delete. I didn't want to keep this message in my inbox. It hurt, because it read like a message of consolation, like he was telling me, "Don't be ashamed, sister, of your US Army uniform. We're all wearing ugly uniforms under our skin." Why did he have to imply that I was ashamed of what I did? Come here and face me, Mr. Muhaymen, and let's compare notes. If you were here, I'd look you straight in the eye and say "I'm not sorry." We came here to do something great and you ruined it. We brought you a basket full of flowers and you vomited all over it. I have nothing more to say. I'm an army interpreter, and that's what I'll remain. I don't want to be your sister, neither by milk nor blood. Wasn't it blood that opened that rift between us, and drove me to say "you and us." I couldn't be anything but American. My Iraqiness had abandoned me long ago. It fell through a hole in my pocket and rolled away like an old coin.

I tried to be both but failed. I took off the khaki and put on the abaya and went to the market in Karada. I bought a loofah and plastic slippers and those chewing gum pieces sold in little bags. I talked to the shopkeeper and teased him in his own accent. He looked at me and smiled encouragingly, like I was some foreign Orientalist.

Now, with the nobility of an older brother, Muhaymen wrote to me to absolve me of the calamities of this war. "You're not responsible for the devastation and lies, Zeina. You're like the rest of us, a victim of lies that are bigger than you."

Delete. I didn't need to be patronized by a hypocritical tribesman who invited me in so that he could clear his throat then offer me protection, swearing by his honor and his moustache, and keeping a knife hidden behind his back. Who was lying to whom, Muhaymen?

I was naive to have imagined democracy to be like candyfloss, colorful sugar wrapped around thin sticks that we could go around distributing to the kids. "What color would you like, *Ammou*?" the nice guy in the democracy van dips the stick in the melted sugar then hands it to the eager child. We sold you a dream that was too good to be true. But we weren't alone. You had your own spin doctors and nuclear scientists and generals. They told us about weapons of mass destruction, about Bin Laden, about a bomb that would finish off Israel. September 11th was waiting for a scapegoat, so we bought it all. You believed us, and we believed them.

Delete. Empty words in the windmill of words.

What good did it do, all this "us and them" analysis?

What use was any of this now, my dear anaemic Sumerian statue?

The last time I saw him was when Tawoos sent for me saying that Nana Rahma was refusing to eat and no longer had the strength to leave her bed. Her health was deteriorating and she wouldn't go to hospital.

When Tawoos asked her, "Do I send for Zeina?," she cursed

me in her Mosul dialect. Tawoos told me my grandfather used to swear a lot, but for my grandmother to swear in the presence of all her saints, the true and the fake, that was unheard of. The virgin looked out of her miracle-working picture whose flame never failed and didn't interfere. I pleaded with Tawoos to tell me what Grandma had said. She told me, like a child repeating something that she knew she wasn't supposed to have heard, covering her mouth with her hand as she said the words, "She said, 'I'll throw her out if I see her, that slut who was raised in the gutter.'" What a *khalooqa*! Another word from my forgotten lexicon that jumped to mind. That's what people in Mosul called a choice swear word: *khalooqa*. My grandmother had sworn, and promised she'd throw me out of her house. I contemplated sending her a doctor from the camp, but feared that he'd receive his own *khalooqa* and also get thrown out. She might even make a scene and invite the neighbors to join in, each with their own *khalooqa*. I knew she'd rather die than let an American examine her, an army doctor at that. But I couldn't take seriously the insults she'd directed at me. I knew I could handle it and take refuge from her in her love for me. I'd take her anger and absorb it. What was the worst she could do?

When I knocked on the door, Haydar opened it and kissed my head. He looked like Muhaymen, just ten years younger. He led me to the inner room. Tawoos was sitting cross-legged on her abaya on the floor by my grandmother's bed and murmuring verses from the Quran while the Virgin Mary listened. "Zeina, you're here." Hope appeared on Tawoos's face as she leaped up to welcome me. My grandmother didn't move. She was awake but her eyes were closed. Her silence encouraged me, so I took off my coat and shoes and snuggled next to her under the covers. She tried to push me away, when I hugged her, but her strength failed her. We stayed like this for a while. Tawoos cried soundlessly in the corner, while Haydar stood chain-smoking just outside the door.

When did Muhaymen get here?

I must've dozed off, engulfed by the warmth and the darkness or the rhythm of Tawoos's sobbing, because I didn't notice him coming in. I smelled him before I saw him, and when I opened my eyes his lean figure was standing over me like a bow drawn taut to shoot an arrow. Was he going to kiss me or strangle me?

How strange the look in his eyes was.

He didn't ask me how I'd gotten there or where I'd been. It was no time for questions. And I was no longer scared. I would extend my hands and surrender to whoever wanted to kidnap me, put a bullet in my head or plant a bomb in my way. What would it change? I'd be just another number in the daily statistics. I was exhausted, and my diary was filling up with the names of dead friends. I didn't want to live like this, with the bitterness on my tongue and the wind of grief blowing through my heart.

I decided to stay the night. At sunset I went out to the garden and picked some oranges to make juice for my grand-mother. I begged her to drink it, invoking the memory of my grandfather and everyone she loved, until she relented and accepted the glass from my hand. Tawoos got up to make us dinner, but wagered me Nana Rahma wouldn't touch it.

There was another power cut. I went outside, and Muhaymen followed me to the small back yard. We sat on the interlaced iron of the rusty old swing, not saying anything at first. I wanted to ask him about the ongoing battles in Sadr City, but I held back. I was sick with worry about him. I followed the news of our soldiers fighting with the Mahdi Army and prayed for *him*, the Iraqi who cut me in two.

"I was very worried about you these past weeks," I finally said.

"Oh, don't worry, you've done your best. You plucked the ripe along with the withered, and the blood you spilled has reached our knees."

He spoke to me as if I were the Pentagon, not Zeina "my dear sister." It hurt.

"Listen, I'm not staying here long. My contract ends in two months."

"But you should stay until the end. Didn't you say that you like movies?"

"This is not the time for jokes."

"You can't run away now, before the scene of your exit from this country."

"Muhaymen, I don't appreciate your tone."

He ignored my protests and started to describe scenes that seemed familiar from another war. The Vietnamese who worked for the US Army hanging on to the wheels of helicopters that took off with the American soldiers and embassy staff, leaving the Vietnamese to their fate.

He didn't call me "dear sister" anymore. Tawoos's milk was spilled in the mire. The war came and sat between us. So the opening scenes were over now, and the real plot was starting. I looked away from him as he continued, "Have you prepared enough helicopters for all the collaborators?"

"Please stop. This hurts."

"That's okay. It won't kill you to hurt a little. Do you know Talib Shannoun? Hassan Abdul-Amir? Muzaffar Al-Shatry? Qais, Hatif, Raad and Abdul-Hussein Al-Nadaf? Those were my friends. They all died under your bombs."

Muhaymen had deceived me with his conciliatory emails, and now he came to exact revenge. It wasn't like me to stay quiet, but I was choking on my replies. Should I ask him about Brian and Jessica and Michael, my friends who were torn apart by mortar shells and roadside bombs?

Muhaymen was attuned to my pain. He could read me, and he showed no mercy.

"Why did you come?"

"We rid you of Saddam."

I knew it was a cliché. I heard myself, and I sounded like a Fox News reporter. The author would certainly edit this out.

Muhaymen came back with a slightly more original line, "You drove King Kong out of the city and claimed the whole of Iraq in return."

XXXV

I wasn't at her house to receive the mourners when she died. I missed my grandmother's wake while I was stuck in the Zone. It was dangerous outside. The city was on fire. Going to her house, and mingling with all the mourners there, would've been an unforgivable breach of security regulations. So I focused on trying to convince Captain Donovan to let me go to the Chaldean cemetery. I said I would follow the funeral procession from a distance. He refused, because the new cemetery was in a faraway suburb.

I played on his emotions. I was aware of how close he'd been to his grandmother who had died a few months back while he was in Baghdad. He'd spent most of his childhood with her after his parents' divorce. We used to listen as he made his phone call to Orange every Sunday after dinner, where it would still be Sunday morning in Connecticut. If he dialed the number and didn't get an answer right away, his face would go pale. He always feared she'd die in her sleep. But Captain Donovan's grandmother didn't die in her sleep. She died a three-hour drive away from her house, by a roulette table at a casino. The little golden ball had stopped on the number she'd put fifty dollars on, and her heart stopped with it. When the news reached Donovan in the Green Zone, so many miles away, we watched him cry and laugh at the same time. The small phone was nearly crushed in his hand as he squeezed it, the way Calvin crushed his beer cans. Donovan finally gave me permission to attend the funeral mass in the church, on the condition that I sit at the back and leave before the ceremony was over. He added that I should take a few soldiers with me and go in a convoy of armored Humvees. But I put my hand up and interrupted him for the first time, "No, sir, forgive me. You gave me permission to go, and I'm not taking anyone with me. I'll take a taxi from the gate. I'll be wearing civilian clothes. I won't attract attention."

As if the roles were reversed, the enlisted interpreter gave orders and the officer obeyed. I wouldn't be able to explain why Donovan agreed. Except that my visible grief seemed to give me a kind of power that superseded military rank. Everyone around me felt it, I think, because they were treating me as if I was some sacred but breakable object, one of those stolen Assyrian sculptures that we sometimes found during the raids. The soldiers would bring it back to the camp, put it on the captain's desk and walk around it, whispering in awe, worried that if they got too close or spoke too loudly the thing would crumble before they'd taken it back to the museum. In a way, I too was a rare object for them. They knew no one else with an Iraqi grandmother who died in Baghdad, because of the heat and the curfew, a half-hour drive away.

My grandmother didn't suffer from a specific illness. "It was grief that killed her," according to Tawoos's prognosis that brooked no doubts. She was rubbing henna into my hair, as I sat cross-legged before her on the warm tiles at the entrance to the bathroom in my grandmother's house when she said, "Nana Rahma will die out of grief."

"She has more strength than both of us. Don't bring her bad luck."

"May she live long, but can't you see how she's wilting? It's out of sadness and humiliation."

Was Tawoos possibly right? Did my grandmother die from the humiliation of my job and my army uniform? Did she die of shame? The shame of an American granddaughter?

Tawoos told me that Rahma had a half-filled bottle of Mistiki Arak that had been my grandfather's. She kept it carefully wrapped in a pillow case and didn't touch it except in extremity.

"My grandmother drinks Arak?" I asked.

"No, but she'd bring the bottle to her nose and breathe in, because the smell reminded her of her husband, then she'd cry and feel better," Tawoos said, then swore by Imam Abbas Abu Fadhil that Rahma drank the whole bottle the day she saw me "wearing American clothes and riding a tank." She spent the whole night wailing like she was mourning a beloved daughter that death took for a bride.

Tawoos must've lost it. She too was getting old and didn't know what she was saying anymore. My grandmother died because she was over eighty years old. Her time was up. It wasn't my fault if someone's time was up.

I put on the black pair of pants that I wore on the way out of Detroit and a black cotton shirt. I wrapped myself in a long raincoat and hid my hair under a generous headscarf. Deborah smiled when she saw me. She waved to me and teased me with a newly acquired Arabic word, "Bye Hajja." I waved feebly back and walked outside with her voice behind me saying "Take care."

It was almost eight in the morning. The overcast sky was the same color as the big concrete barriers at the gate. I hailed a taxi and asked the driver to take me to Saint Joseph Church in Eastern Karada. He drove off, and I sat in the back covering my face with my hand and letting my tears flow like rain after a drought.

The driver shouted, "It's the American bastards, isn't it? I wouldn't wish it on anyone to be at their mercy." He must have thought I was disappointed by a failed petition or something. I didn't reply. I wiped my face and nose with the edge of my headscarf and asked him to hurry because I had to be at a funeral. He didn't seem moved, as if the people of Baghdad only left their homes to go to funerals. It was daily routine, no different from going to the cinema in happier lands.

I thought about what I'd find when I got there. Who would come? Would the funeral proceed in peace? If it was up to me I would've arranged for military protection, but Rahma might have risen from her coffin to spit on us. My love for her shouldn't tarnish her last moments on this earth.

I started crying again, and the driver continued pouring his curses on the head of the occupation and the "black day" that brought the Americans to the country. "Sister, don't cry. Thank your God that you're walking on two legs. Yesterday I carried two women to the Emergency, and they'd both lost their legs in an explosion on the bus. One of them died before we'd made it to the hospital."

When I got to church, the body was already there. I saw the funeral car outside the high iron gates. My tears wouldn't stop. I walked over a large puddle of slippery mud, leaped onto the sidewalk, then ran up the steps to the church's main door. There was a power cut, and the churchwardens probably didn't want to use the generator for a quick minor ceremony. None of the old woman's children were here to pay generously—they were all abroad. So candles were both cheaper and more atmospheric.

The darkness helped me. I walked on tiptoe down the side aisle and settled between the black-clad women in the first two rows. The other rows were empty. I wasn't going to sit at the back. I was the only granddaughter she had present here. I stayed focused on the shiny wooden box and the gold crucifix that adorned it. I didn't look at the faces of the women around me. There was no time for social pleasantries. The coffin was placed on a plinth draped in blue velvet, three wreaths of plastic flowers leaning on either side of it. I tried to pierce the wood and get to my grandmother's skin. I didn't like it when they tied the hands of the dead to their sides. If she were free she would've hugged me.

The old priest encircled the coffin with an incense holder swinging at the end of a thick chain and releasing puffs of white smoke. The fragrance reached me quickly.

"Qadisha Alaha, Qadisha Hilthana, Qadisha Lamayotha. God's mercy be on her," went the Chaldean prayer the priest was chanting.

Women were blowing their noses loudly into their handkerchiefs, their chests rising and falling with each sigh, their bodies swaying back and forth to the rhythm of the chant. The two young deacons followed the priest and repeated the prayers after him. To be here they'd had to get up early and venture into streets that had turned into human traps. Their eyes scanned the mourners for a young face that might have made the risk worthwhile.

My sobs were getting louder. A chubby older woman turned towards me. Her face was still pretty despite her age, and the memory tape turned in my head until I realized she was my Uncle Munir's wife. Apparently a similar tape was turning in her head, because she peered at me closely and with growing surprise. Then, in a heavy Mosul accent with its guttural "r," she said, "Who? Zeina? Batoul's daughte*gh*? When did you a*gh*ive from ab*gh*oad? Come he*ghe*, my dea*gh* and let me kiss you! May Allah have me*gh*cy on your *ggh*andma's soul. It would have made he*gh* so happy to see you."

One by one the women forgot about the body of my grand-mother laid out by the altar. They left their places on the narrow benches and came to me, repeating my name in whispered tones and taking turns hugging and kissing me. Their kisses were properly wet and noisy and did not go to waste in the air, but left their marks on my skin. Their lips were like suction cups that stuck to my cheek and absorbed my grief. Their tears caressed my face, and my tears moved to their tired cheeks that were so used to that particular moisture, as if they'd long been addicted to the saltiness of tears. Women here took their crying seriously. It was a way of life, an exercise they did regularly, individually and in groups, to stay spiritually fit. Crying strengthened the heart muscle and lowered the blood pressure. It sometimes had an intoxicating effect not unlike that of beer. I watched the teardrops suspended on the tips of their noses and remembered that I hadn't had a good cry since childhood. I'd had a moderate life, with no extremes of sadness or joy.

The priest spoke sternly, "Shush. Some respect for the dead, please."

The commotion caused by my magical appearance in the church subsided. The two young deacons resumed their chanting while looking at me with friendly curiosity. I was a new face in the congregation. Stories would be woven around me, speculation and gossip. Soon the link would be made to the story of my parents. The Chaldean girl who opposed her family to marry an Assyrian. The man was later arrested and then they fled to America. But what brought the daughter back?

As if by a miracle, like the ones that Grandma used to order from her saints, I was turned into a member of the congregation under the gaze of the women and the deacons. There were so many sects springing up in the country nowadays. You had to be with one or the other. But if you asked Tawoos, she'd tell you that I was a dog with two homes.

Eventually I'd have to slip out of the church and away from the sect, leaving Rahma Girgis Saour asleep in her wooden box. My sadness was like a presence that walked out with me, protecting me from the rain and humming in my ears.

I wanted Muhaymen to be here so I could cry on his shoulder, like women do.

He and Tawoos were probably trapped in Sadr. Was the massacre there not over yet?

XXXVI

It tasted like vinegar. Freedom in this country tasted like vinegar. Bush was sad about the four thousand American soldiers who were killed in Iraq. He said that he thought a lot about every single one of them. Our poor president. How could he possibly hold four thousand distinct thoughts in his head? I didn't want to add to his intellectual difficulties by becoming number four thousand and one. No, I hadn't come to my birthplace to die, just to fall in love with a Mission Impossible man. Well, unrequited love was another kind of death.

It was 25 March 2008. The date appeared on the corner of my laptop screen. My second contract with the army had come to an end and I hadn't renewed it. Here's what I have brought back from Baghdad: a sadness like pure honey, thick and sticky and translucent, good for insomnia and poetry, bad for my ageing skin and my aching joints. It was the kind of suffering that lifts you up and weighs you down. It took me by the hand, led me to a forest of gray trees and left me there.

I decided: no souvenirs, no tears, no final glances at a house, bridge, or palm tree. I am still dealing with the burden of my grandmother's memory. We barely had time to talk. My visits to her were furtive, stolen from the war. Her project of my re-education was never completed, but what she'd given me had completed me as a woman, as a human being.

How are we supposed to preserve the living memories of the dead? If we let their experiences go with them to the grave, they're lost to us for good. And then we must go back to the start and get our fingers burned as we relearn everything. We crawl like infants and bump into things, but insist that we know it all. We rely on mystics and novelists to tell us our own history. There's no memory bank for this kind of data.

In a science fiction version of my life, I'd have plugged a memory stick into my grandmother's head, copied her memory onto it, then plugged it into my own temple and clicked copy and paste. Within seconds, her wisdom and experience would have been transferred to my brain. What do we call this gadget in Arabic again? The Keeper of Memory.

I'm tired. And my laptop is tired of me and of my writer alter ego who would have followed me to Detroit if I'd let her. She would have liked to record my downfall, then she would've gotten up from her writing table, stretched her arms and back, clapped in delight and poured herself a drink to celebrate her victory over the American granddaughter. But she too has changed since the day we first met. I no longer see her in colorful shirts and a modern haircut. The story has turned her, chapter after chapter, into an old-fashioned woman with values that time has forgotten. Does time really forget? She dresses like the women from Falluja now. Her face has the sharp features of the women of Mosul, who, by the way, would all, every single one of them, make excellent school mistresses or matrons. They're all hardworking, frugal, uncompromising. If you say to one of them, "Come on, some give and take, let's negotiate a middle ground," she shakes her head resolutely and marches on.

I didn't wait around for the author to take off her abaya and dance on my grave. I didn't stay until the day that Muhaymen anticipated, the day of the fleeing helicopters. I arranged a roadside bomb for the author instead. I killed her off before she could kill me. Now I'm sitting alone, in front of my screen, finishing my story.

When I left Iraq, I didn't go straight home. I flew into Washington and went to visit the Arlington Cemetery. I looked for Regina Barnhurst, but didn't find her in front of the marble headstone. It was getting cold by the time I found Brian's grave. Leesa Philippon saw me from a distance, came over and put a hand on my shoulder. I recognized her from the photo in the paper. I had it stored in a picture folder on my computer that I used every now and then to sharpen the arrow tips of my sadness. Leesa looked like she lived in the cemetery. She keeps the absent boys company and wipes the snow off their graves. She protects the bones of the dead from the cold. The mothers have received their compensation money, and their fingers still burn from its touch.

"Was it a father or a husband that you lost?"

Would Leesa believe me if I told her that I had lost my author and a part of myself? She invited me to join her club, but I couldn't belong to anything anymore, not even to my own name. The woman who owned all my nicknames—Zuwayna, Zayoun, Zonzon—was gone. Was there a club for granddaughters in mourning?

Back at the airport I bought a mug printed with 20.01.09, Bush's last day in office. He'd go, all right, but his curse would remain, polluting the waters of the two rivers for generations to come. They'd call it the curse of Bush, like the curse of the pharaohs. I think Americans will call it that too, and NASA will have to send out space missions in search of a curse-free galaxy.

I got home and took a long shower. But the dust of sorrow didn't come off and flow down the drain with the soap. It stuck to me like another layer of skin. It stayed to complete the project of my re-education. It's there when I drive around in my car, when I see people laughing, shopping, eating and putting on weight. Do these people know what I've been through? Do they know what's still going on over there? Our sons and daughters in the army have become mute numbers who carry their tombstones on their shoulders as they walk.

I don't think I need psychological counseling like others who've returned from Iraq. My sorrow is taking good care of me. I won't be committing suicide like my friend Sad Malek, the British lord from Basra. "We ate shit, Zeina my dear." He took a car and left Mosul, heading south. They later say that he intended to return to his city and disappear there. Or that he was following Sayyab to Jekor, the poet's birthplace. But he never made it. His car went off the road and into a palm tree. Eyewitnesses say the driver waved to them before driving the car at full speed into the line of palm trees. Malek had had enough of eating shit and was going to nibble on dates with the angels instead.

I put my khaki uniform in a plastic bag and threw it out with the garbage. I won't be planting basil in my helmet. Sweet perfume doesn't grow in metal. That's what I write to Muhaymen, but he doesn't reply. Bombs are still falling over there, and I guess internet cafés offer little protection.

So in the end, I left alone. Haydar didn't come with me. Muhaymen stayed behind and I've made him into my Keeper of Sorrows.

I brought no gifts and no keepsakes. I need no reminders. I just repeat after my father: I'd give my right hand if I should ever forget you, Baghdad.

A NOTE ON THE TRANSLATOR

Nariman Youssef is a London-based literary translator and translation consultant in the arts and culture sector.